SPEAKING IN TONGUES

A COLLECTION OF ORIGINAL
SHORT STORIES BY

KEVIN JOHN WINDORF

I0532718

QUINDORIAN PRESS

10th Anniversary Edition

Cover photo by Bill Lavelle.
Cover design by Kevin Windorf.
Author photo by Jim Richards.

Lyrics from
"Meant To Be" written by Mary Fahl
© 2013 Mary Fahl
used with permission.
www.maryfahl.com

ISBN: 0615900321
ISBN-13: 978-0615900322 (Quindorian Press)

ALSO BY KEVIN JOHN WINDORF

The Gate
The Serpent Bearer: 13 Stories of Suspense
Call From The Cabin
The Depth of My Drink, collected poems

www.kevinwindorf.com

Above its sad and lowly plains
They bend on hovering wing,
And ever o'er its Babel sounds
The blessed angels sing.

— Edmund Hamilton Sears

STORIES & TALES

SPEAKING IN TONGUES

Outside of Babel, the small two-story building sat by itself at the intersection of County Road 14, which ran mostly east west, and Route 5, a north south artery that saw a lot more traffic 20 miles north and 30 miles south. Around Babel, Route 5 was simply "the Boulevard" as if it was something grand, or, like the small two-story building, something someone had once hoped would be grand.

David Burns had bought the land on what would become the southeast corner of the intersection as soon as plans for the new Route 5 were announced, some three generations past. His thought was to build the finest roadhouse this side of the desert. His dream did come true, for about a three-year stretch, when his "Boulevard Saloon" did in fact become a destination for locals within a 30-mile radius, as well as for the steady stream of thirsty travelers who came along the new road.

He made the second floor his home, with a few bedrooms and a full kitchen and bath. The building had a pitched roof of cedar shingle that made it look homey, despite the neon sign that spelled out Boulevard Saloon in three-foot-high letters that ran the length of the building. You couldn't miss that sign if you were driving by. It kind of made one thirsty.

Mr. Burns might have been a visionary, but he fell short of being a good businessman, and proved to have no imagination when it came to running a roadhouse, at least in a style that would keep regular customers coming back and new folks seeking it out.

When times got tough, he'd rent out a room or two upstairs, sometimes just for a night – usually if a fellow had too many drinks or too many words with a fed-up wife. The rooms were strictly off-limits for any type of extra-curricular activity, as Mr. Burns was a church-going, God-fearing, tax-paying prude.

About five years after the business at Boulevard Saloon peaked, Mr. Burns up and died, as they say, and, confirming the talk behind his back about his limited business acumen, he left no will. But that wasn't too much of a problem since there were no heirs. Still, when the bank seized the building and land, there was just no one interested in taking over the Boulevard Saloon and taking on the task of resurrecting Mr. Burns' vision. So a generation passed before the building was bought and re-opened, and since then, it's been "just a bar" with no grand aspirations beyond being an air-conditioned oasis where locals can stop in for a beer, a conversation with acquaintances, a game of billiards or darts and a loud song on the jukebox.

But no one calls it Boulevard Saloon anymore. One day the neon word "Boulevard" up and disappeared, as they say, leaving just the orangey red glow of "Saloon," which could still be seen for quite a stretch in any direction away from the intersection.

The current proprietor, one Thomas T. Thomas, inherited the establishment from an uncle on his mother's side, a drifter (perhaps grifter is more accurate) named Harold Diebold. Harry liked to tell how he won the deed to the Saloon in a backroom poker game, but that was just one of his fictions that no one believed, not so much because it was unbelievable, but because no one cared.

Truth was that Harry bought it from the local bank, who had foreclosed on the prior owner, an Elizabeth Smythe Hightower, who was a middle-aged stable widow when she first took ownership of the Saloon, not so stable when she decided to stop serving alcohol some 14 years later, and not so middle-aged when she left Babel in the back of an ambulance. No one seemed to remember how she came to own the Saloon in the first place, not because it was any big mystery, but because no one cared.

What folks around did care about was that the Saloon was open for business, served alcohol, and the proprietor Thomas T. Thomas kept it clean, kept the beer cold, kept the jukebox up to date (but not at the sacrifice of some old favorites), and kept the prices reasonable. He had all the signs of being a fair and decent barkeep, and he had the respect, if not admiration, of his clientele. But what he didn't have was the tip of his tongue. And that's why, despite the obvious expectations, the Saloon wasn't called "Tommy's" or "Tom-Tom's" or "The Triple T." It was called, by the regulars anyway, "Tongue's." And Mr. Thomas was called to his face "Tongue," not a particularly charming moniker, but not by far the worst nickname uttered about other residents in the Babel community.

Now how Mr. Thomas came to lose the tip of his tongue is one of those mysteries people wonder about for the better part of a minute, and then move on with their lives. Perhaps disappointed in the deficiency of attention, Tongue was known to weave a wide assortment of little vignettes to explain away his missing ounce of flesh. Sometimes the tales would take on a bigger-than-life tragic tableau with the loss of only a small part of his tongue to be quite a relief to Mr. Thomas. But more often than not, Tongue would seek out compassion from his clientele by offering self-deprecating stories of mishap and human error that made him out to be no better, and no less lucky, than the next fellow. Mostly, people would smile politely and order another round.

One Saturday afternoon, a quiet fellow sitting at the bar by himself – a shaggy dog professor type, perhaps taking the Boulevard north to one of those colleges near the coast – found himself listening to Tongue's latest tale, which, on that day, involved being sliced by a machete-wielding angry father of a young Panamanian lady he was "getting to know" when he was in the Peace Corps. The professor took it all in with an emphatic "Hunh." Then he smiled politely and ordered another mug of beer.

When Tongue deposited the frosty glass in front of him on a cocktail napkin, the professor put the glass aside and flipped the napkin onto the dry side. Taking a ballpoint from his jacket pocket, he began to draw on the napkin, saying to Tongue, "So you're just like Mick Jagger."

"He was in the Peace Corps?"

"Maybe. But I don't think so."

"What do you mean then?"

The professor smiled at Tongue. "Mick Jagger, you know, the singer from The Rolling Stones. He lost the tip of his tongue, too. At least, that's what they say."

"Whoa. No way." Tongue was genuinely dumbfounded. Sure he knew The Stones and Mick Jagger. "Start Me Up" was B17 on the jukebox and typically got play any Friday night when a big group of guys – or gals – would come in, looking for a big night at the bar.

Tongue leaned in and asked almost conspiratorially, "How did he lose it?"

"Oh, I'm sure he has stories, too." With that, the professor presented his finished drawing to Tongue. On the napkin, he had drawn the famous Rolling Stones logo, the big smiling lips with the exposed tongue. Except, instead of a plump round tip, the professor truncated the tongue with a squared off end.

"That's excellent! I love it." Tongue was quite amused. And so was the professor, who finished his beer, and moved on with his life, never giving thought again to his artwork or to visiting the roadside bar in Babel, completely unaware of his impact on the bartender's life.

One month later, Tongue received a shipment of two boxes from an out-of-state company he'd found on the Internet. The larger box contained 100 white t-shirts with a big red image of the professor's clipped tongue logo.

Arcing above the shiny-looking lips was the word "TONGUES" printed in all upper-case black letters. Matching the letters, in a mirrored arc below the lips, was the word "SALOON."

The smaller box contained 500 cardboard coasters, all imprinted with the makeshift logo: red lips, clipped tongue, "TONGUES SALOON."

The day Tongue received the boxes, Francis Everett, the UPS man who'd had Babel on his route for the better part of 10 years, decided to stick around and see what his delivery was all about. He wasn't being nosey, just neighborly. He couldn't remember ever making a delivery at the Saloon, but he'd been an occasional customer, and he felt a certain obligation to share in customers' excitement about getting something by post. Oftentimes his customers were so jubilant to get what they were getting, they'd brag to Francis what was in the box, ripping it open in front of him, just to show off the merchandise purchased, the keepsake sent by family, or the whatnot that somehow would make someone's day a little bit better.

And that was the case with Tongue. He was so giddy in getting the double box delivery and seeing that Francis was looking to stick around – it was before noon on a Tuesday – Tongue poured him a cold draft without even asking first.

"You see it? You see it?" Tongue was spreading out a t-shirt on the bar for Francis to appraise. Then he dropped two coasters on top, to drive the point across. "The logo! Get it?"

Francis sipped his beer. "Sure do." Francis sipped his beer some more.

Tongue just couldn't stop smiling. "You see what it's missing?"

"Yep."

"The tip of the tongue. The tip of the tongue. Just like me."

"Yep. And the apostrophe."

Tongue's smile pulled back across his face like a metal measuring tape retreating into its case. "The what?"

Patiently, Francis Everett, a veteran of thousands upon thousands of UPS deliveries, explained how "TONGUES" should have been spelled as "TONGUE'S." He cited his experience in reading countless addresses over the years, as well as his deep interest in military history and military fiction, which added up somehow to Francis being something of an expert when it came to punctuation. Frankly, Tongue didn't see the connection, but more importantly, he didn't see that Francis was right.

With the air out of his balloon, so to speak, Tongue felt far less animated, and far less generous. He noticed Francis' glass was empty. "You want to run a tab?"

"Nah, best be going. What will you do with the shirts?"

"Thought I'd sell them."

"Discount for the typo?"

"Damn, Francis. Do you think people are going to notice?"

Francis gave him a big smile. "I'm sure they will. But frankly…" He leaned over the bar to continue in his own conspiratorial whisper, "… they won't give a …" even softer, "… rat's ass."

With a quick wink, Francis was out the door, "Thanks for the beer, Mr. Thomas T. Thomas," calling Tongue by his proper name, because that's how the boxes were addressed.

That night, Tongue had a few t-shirts on display behind the bar, and he used the coasters with every new drink he served. He gave a t-shirt to Marilu, the college graduate who waited tables on weekends, and asked her to wear it, "sort of as a uniform." She obliged, but because the Large was way too large for her slight physique (Tongue had ordered only Larges and Extra Larges), she tied a knot in the shirt above her right hip. As a result, the logo was twisted across her chest, and the image and letters couldn't be deciphered. It upset Tongue, but he wouldn't have Marilu undo the knot, since the tightness of the shirt was more likely to sell drinks than his logo would. He did resolve to add the logo to the back of the shirt on his next order, once he sold out of the 90 tees stacked neatly under the bar, next to the crate of never-used martini glasses.

Marilu happily distributed the coasters with each order, and eventually, people would ask her, polite and unsure, "Shouldn't there be an apostrophe?" She would just wink and serve the drinks with a smile.

Tongue was a satisfied man, feeling a surging identity for his establishment. He fancied himself becoming a local celebrity – and that was something to hang his hat on.

Tongue's Tale 1

Let me tell you how I really lost the tip of my tongue...

    I was born and raised in Hawaii and never saw snow for real until my family moved to Alaska to mine for gold. Well, seeing an icicle hanging from my window was the damned most beautiful thing I'd ever seen. Of course, I was only six at the time and hadn't seen much. But I just grabbed that icicle, must have been a foot long, and I gave a long slow lick... well you know the rest.

SWAMP (7:05 PM)

It was the Saturday night of Labor Day weekend. Tongue was restocking bottles of beer in the refrigerator below the bar and his back was turned to the front door, but when he heard it open, he peeked at the digital clock next to the register. The red LED numbers confirmed it was 7:05. "Hey there, Geoff."

"Evening, Mr. Thomas."

Tongue knew the first customer of the night would be Old Man Geoffrey Jefferies, who came in every Friday and Saturday night between 7 and 7:05 like clockwork. The old man and Tongue had gotten along since the night they first met – the Friday night Tongue re-opened the Saloon. Upon introduction Tongue realized that they shared the uncommon amusement (or curse) of sharing one name for first and last.

"Geoffrey Jefferies? Ain't that something? I'm Thomas Thomas," Tongue had explained. "I have the same first and last name, too."

"Well, good for you, boy. But my names are different, Geoffrey and Jefferies. Besides one's a G and t'other's a J. Couldn't be more different."

Tongue realized he was pulling his leg some. "Whatever you say, my friend. What can I get you to drink?"

And here's where another legend began. Geoff asked for a Drambuie, his favorite potent potable, which he drank every night of his adult life – five nights a week at home, two nights at the Saloon (when it was open and serving liquor). He believed the honey-infused elixir, drunk in moderation (two full glasses, on the rocks, per night), was the perfect medicinal remedy for a long life that was not aligning conveniently with a love life.

Unfortunately, Tongue misheard Geoff's order, and thought he asked for a Jim Bowie, whatever that might be. "A Jim Bowie? You mean like the knife?"

"What knife?" Geoff was equally bewildered.

A few more exchanges and they had it worked out, but, alas, Tongue didn't stock Drambuie (having never heard of it). Geoff left amid a barrage of uttered disgruntlement, but not before Tongue vowed to get a bottle by the next night, which he did. And Old Man Jefferies did return, took his stool, was greeted by Tongue and the desired drink, at exactly 7:05. A routine was established for Tongue and re-instituted for Geoffrey.

Old Man Jefferies was the only customer who'd been coming to the Saloon since before Tongue's Uncle Harry owned it. Geoff might have been younger than he looked, but Tongue guessed he was nearing 70. He was definitely retired. From what, Geoff would never say. But he came to Babel in the late 80s, back when Elizabeth Smythe Hightower was pouring the draughts and concoctions she'd ultimately label "demon rum" in a sweeping generalization. During the time that the bank – First National Bank of Babel, that is – foreclosed on Miss Elizabeth and shut the Saloon down, Geoff stayed home for his Drambuie. Once Harry Diebold came to town, however, Geoff reacquainted himself with his Friday night-Saturday night bar stool.

Although he had been a regular customer of Harry Diebold, Geoff never spoke of him. Except one Thanksgiving Friday, when he stopped in for his usual tumbler of "Jim Bowie" (which he and Tongue came to call the requested beverage) and recollected a story to Tongue about his uncle.

"Had a turkey shoot out back."

Tongue was busy drying a rack of freshly washed glasses. Towel in hand, he moved along the bar to get closer to the conversation. "What do you mean? He shot a turkey?"

Old Man Jefferies looked hard at Tongue. "You pulling my leg or you just stupid? Turkey shoot is a shootin' contest. Shoot a gun, win a turkey. Not shoot a turkey, win a gun. Though that's not a bad idea."

"What happened?"

"Your Uncle Harry set up a contest, out back, behind the parking lot. Pay two bucks, take one shot, with *his* gun. If you hit the target, you win a turkey. For Thanksgiving."

"Sounds like fun. What was the target?"

"Empty liquor bottle."

"Did you win?"

Old Man Jefferies didn't blink but his face showed a sign of amazement. He let some disappointment pour forth. "No, I didn't win. Nobody won."

"Why not?"

"Because your uncle was a cheat. He wouldn't let us use our own guns. Had to use his rifle."

Tongue stopped drying glasses so he could concentrate. He felt he was missing something. "So?"

"So?! Harry Diebold was a cheat. He made sure that the sights on his gun were off. No one could hit nothing."

"If the sights were off, why didn't you just take another shot, adjusting for the difference."

"Bah." Geoffrey waved his hand in dismissal at Tongue. "Had to pay a second time. No one wanted to do that and miss again. It was only a damn turkey. Diebold hadn't even bought the turkey, he just collected the money. Took us a while to realize what he was up to. Real nice guy your uncle."

"Okay, but I'm not my uncle."

Old Man Jefferies just stared at him and sipped his

Drambuie, thinking, 'what's the use,' and never mentioned Harry Diebold again to anyone.

On the Saturday night of Labor Day weekend, Old Man Jefferies took to his perch on the stool at the elbow of the bar, as expected. He liked sitting there because it gave him "easy viewing of everything I need to see," he explained once to Marilu, the college grad who worked weekend nights as the Saloon's only waitress.

"I can see all along the bar. See who's drinking what. I got the best view of the TVs, and I'm close enough to hear the damn things if there was ever any reason to turn up the volume. Mirror gives me a peek at everything going on at the tables, not that there's a damn thing ever going on. And this seat is the furthest I can get from that jukebox racket."

Marilu, who was in charge of selecting the music for the jukebox, was about to walk away feeling slighted, when Old Man Jefferies added, "But the main reason I always sit here is so I can be next to you whenever you come up for your drink orders." He winked at her.

Marilu gave him a little squeeze on his forearm, "That's so sweet." Then she walked away and went on with her night, wondering who she'd be when she was old.

Because it was a Saturday night, Jed Ellison came into the bar at 8:20. Didn't matter it was Labor Day weekend, when most residents of Babel left town. Jed never went away. He ran the local hardware store, Harrison's. Harrison was a name that went back to the founding of the town, and there were many places named Harrison throughout it. There was Harrison Avenue, Harrison Street and Harrison Court, there was Harrison's Diner, Harrison Park, and the Harrison Memorial Library, and a few lesser spots. So everyone just called things what they were: the library, the park, the diner, etc. That's why Jed was the owner of just "the hardware store." The one exception of course was Harrison's Liquor Store, which was called Harrison's. That wasn't surprising to the folks in town, because no one ever liked saying they were going to the liquor store. Going to the Saloon? Perfectly fine. Acceptable. Understood. Perhaps admired. Going to the liquor store? That was bad. Meant there was trouble at home, scandal, infidelity, immorality, or even elitism. It would be seriously frowned upon and might result in tongue-clicking. What was surprising to the townsfolk was that the town wasn't called Harrison. Why it was called Babel was a bit of a mystery, one that the town librarian, Priscilla Waymore tried to investigate but failed. She poured through every record of local history and spoke to every old timer still alive in Babel. She covered what she imagined was every possible resource, but the origin of the name Babel had apparently never been recorded and no one could remember knowing why. Priscilla was quite disappointed – not because she couldn't determine the origin of Babel's naming, but because no one seemed to care.

At precisely 8:00 pm on Saturday nights, Jed Ellison locked the front door of the hardware store, without fail. By 8:20, he was walking through the Saloon doors, heading for his perch next to Old Man Jefferies, without fail. Except one time, when a bus heading north on Route 5 stopped in town because the bus driver had gotten lost. The passengers, 36 women of various ages, heading to a county fair singing competition on the other side of the mountains, demanded that the bus driver let them get refreshments at the Saloon. Not only did they commandeer all the bar stools – except for the one where Old Man Jefferies was already safely parked – but they dominated the tables as well. They promised the bus driver they'd stay for only one round, but, no surprise, they stayed for three. Marilu and Tongue had never been so busy in such a short span of time.

The ladies just loved the music on the jukebox, and being semi-professional singers, they sang along with each selection they made, loud and proud, like it was their own concert. They also loved the Tongues Saloon logo. All of them bought t-shirts regardless of shirt size, except the two oldest of the ladies, who found the logo offensive, and the three youngest – who were still minors by a year – because the other ladies thought the logo inappropriate for "our little ones." At least half the ladies "stole" logo-ed coasters to take as souvenirs.

Once they were gone, Tongue and Marilu realized that Jed had come in and sat at a back table and had been completely ignored. Welcoming him up to the bar stool next to Old Man Jefferies, Tongue said, "First one's on me." Marilu squeezed Jed's forearm, "I'm so sorry, sweetie." Then she walked away and bussed the tables, wondering what she'd do if she were ever alone on a Saturday night.

But the Saturday night of Labor Day weekend would find a lighter crowd than usual, because of the loss of vacationers. Jed took his seat next to Old Man Jefferies and ordered his first beer.

"Good day?" asked Geoff between sips of his Jim Bowie.

"Sure was, Geoff, sure was."

"Why's that?"

"Labor Day." Jed gave an expansive smile and clapped his hand on Geoff's shoulder. "Anyone who doesn't go away feels an obligation to do some work on his house." He toasted his imagined customers with the beer glass Tongue just delivered. "Or on the front yard. Or the backyard."

Geoff said barely aloud, "I don't feel any such obligation."

"Don't have a house, now, do you?" Jed whispered in a friendly kidding way.

Geoff whispered back, without the charm, "Don't have any friends, now, do you?"

"Ah, don't say that, Old Man Jefferies." Jed clapped

his shoulder again. "I've got you."

"Queer."

"Hey, that's not funny."

"That's the truth." Geoff took a longer draw from his drink.

Jed took a minute to gaze around the Saloon. No crowd to speak of yet, but he'd expect that for the holiday weekend. Just of table of ten, mostly women. But it was still early, he thought. Tongues usually peaked after 9, then settled down by 11. The pattern might have been developed over time by the Saturday night ritual of a drink after a movie date, getting home on time for the babysitter, and just folks being careful to not have too many before getting behind the wheel. Whatever reasons got fed into the creature, the result was a living biorhythm that took control for the better part of two hours and brought more life to the sleepy town than any other night – with the only exception being Christmas Midnight Mass at the Roman Catholic Church, St. Jerome's, which was known far and wide for some great choral and organ performances that brought in worshippers of all faiths who just wanted to breathe in a bit of holiday spirit.

Jed looked back at Old Man Jefferies. He couldn't remember seeing him at Midnight Mass. Nor could he remember a Saturday night that didn't find Geoff on his perch, though he'd be gone before his self-imposed 9 pm bewitching hour. "So, what are you doing this weekend, Geoff?"

"What?"

"This weekend. Got any plans?"

"Yep."

"Well, what are you planning on doing?"

"I'm doing it."

"Come on. Aren't you gonna have a big barbecue in your backyard, invite all the neighbors and their kids over to your place for some good old, you know, fun?"

Old Man Jefferies turned and stared hard at Jed.

"Always was a wise ass. How do you stay in business?"

Jed met the grizzled look with his typical smile. "Charm. And screws. I sell a lot of screws." He winked at Geoff.

"Not surprised. Lots of people in this town have loose screws."

"True, true."

Geoff took the last gulp of his Drambuie. Tongue served it on the rocks with a slice of orange, just the way Old Man Jefferies demanded a few years back when Tongue first took over. Tongue didn't use an orange in another single drink, but he always made sure he had one on hand for Friday and Saturday nights, for Old Man Jefferies' nightly order – "Drambuie. Rocks. Orange" – as if he even needed to say anything. Tongue knew he'd arrive between "seven and seven o five," be done with his first by 7:45, order the second around 8, finish it by 8:30, but sit for another 30 minutes. Then Old Man Jefferies would pay his tab and leave a dollar tip for Tongue.

Jed and Tongue would usually share a few words about Old Man Jefferies after he left. They enjoyed his company, respected his opinions, learned a few things now and again, but mostly they were amused by the regimen of his social comings and goings. If Fourth of July fell on a Friday, Saturday, or Sunday, Old Man Jefferies would stay for a third round, and head home by 10. Jed and Tongue deduced that Old Man Jefferies' interest – or tolerance – in staying later on an Independence Day weekend hinted that he had been in the military. But the one time Jed asked if he had been, his response had been a curt "Hunh."

On the Saturday night of Labor Day weekend, Old Man Jefferies looked into his empty glass and swirled the ice. Something was on his mind, Jed thought.

"You plan on working the hardware store your whole life?" Geoff asked him.

Oh, this again, thought Jed. "Not my whole life, just

till I retire."

"Let me tell you something, boy. Men working in a hardware store is like a woman working in a library. They turn out spinsters. Unhappy. Own lots of cats. Wasted life." He looked at Jed. "Screws. I doubt that."

Jed clapped his hand onto Geoff's shoulder, in a friendly manner, but his tone got all serious. "Geoff, let me ask you. What you got against cats?"

After a pause both men cackled. "Good one!" Geoff clinked his glass against Jed's pint of beer and slurped down the drop of remnant water at the bottom of his "Jim Bowie."

Suddenly he caught a line of conversation from two men who were seated a few stools away, just on the other side of the taps. "Psst." Geoff got their attention and toasted them with his empty glass, "Drambuie is from Scotland."

Tongue, standing by the men, said to Geoff, with a big foolish smile, "But not Jim Bowie. He was from Kentucky."

'Bah,' Geoff thought to himself. It was time to go, he knew, so he got up and stood next to Jed's stool. The two of them looked eye to eye. "Let me tell you something about life, young fella. Life is like a swamp. When you're not looking, it will grow all around you, slowly take you over. Cut you off, choke you to death, smother you in ways you can't know. Then you wake up one day and say, I don't have my own life, I have a swamp. And it'll be too late. You got to do something with your life to keep the swamp out."

The import of Old Man Jefferies' words was not lost on Jed, and he recognized the wisdom and a sense of regret that informed Geoff's words. But he was mostly struck by Geoff's motivation to share this life-saving advice with Jed. In a way Jed was touched. But he couldn't let the old man slide, getting all personal like that, all of a sudden.

Jed spoke kindly to him. "What you say, my friend, might be true. But the swamp is nature. Life is natural. Let it be and it will take care of you. If you fight the swamp, if you fill your life with... stuff. The things that distract a man. The things that blind him to the beauty of life. Well then, all you're doing is fighting the swamp with landfill. And the landfill of life is just man-made garbage. You don't want a life of landfill."

"Jed, I don't know what you're saying. But it sounds like garbage to me. Do me a favor, next time you sell someone a box of screws, keep a few for yourself."

"Home safe, Geoff."

"Hunh." Old Man Jefferies slapped his money on the bar and headed out the door. Passing Marilu, he shot her a smile and a slight bow of his head. She winked back, and he left a happy man for yet another night.

Tongue's Tale 2

I used to have this big bushy moustache. I know it's hard to imagine me with a moustache. Just trust me that at the time it was quite, well, let's say, fashionable. Anyway, the point is that one day I decided it wasn't fashionable anymore and it needed to come off. Now the great irony of my story is that I didn't want to cut it off myself because I was afraid I might nick myself. If only.

So, I went to Vinny's Barbershop, where's I'd been getting my hair cut since I moved to Babel. Old Vincenzo who ran the place was old when I met him. I never had any problems before. But the day I showed up to get my moustache cut off, Vincenzo was sporting a new pair of eyeglasses. Coke bottles really. Claimed that the new eye doctor in town recommended a drastically new prescription. Who am I to question men of science? Anyway, just as Vincenzo placed his big scissors under my nose, it tickled, and I just instinctively stuck my tongue out to lick at my lip. Boy there was a lot of blood. Old Vincenzo never opened his shop again, and that eye doctor was never seen again in Babel. True story.

PULL UP THE ROOTS (8:30 PM)

"I have to admit, this is quite a milestone for me. I mean, besides being here with you, which is a milestone in its own right." Peg looked around the Saloon like a tourist returning to a favorite vacation spot, trying to determine what she remembered and what looked new.

Colin also gazed around, but more like a student sneaking into the faculty lounge. "I've been looking forward to having my first drink in the Saloon, well, it feels like my whole life."

"Exciting, isn't it?"

"Now don't take this the wrong way, but I never thought my first excursion inside the Saloon would be with my mom."

"Oh, I do understand that, Colin. You'd be crazy to think otherwise."

Peg assessed her 21 year old son in the manner which was typical for her. She measured him through her. What did she look like when she was 21? What was she thinking about the most when she had that big birthday (bearing in mind that for her, the legal drinking age had been 18)? What was the next step in her life?

Well, naturally she thought she had looked better then than Colin looked now, not that she was being critical, just observant. She knew she'd always been pretty, and healthy looking. She was outdoorsy and athletic, maybe with a streak of the tomboy. Colin wore more stress on his face than she ever did or would. He was a worrier, a bit of a loner. No, that was harsh, Peg corrected herself. He's just shy. But that he got from his father.

And that's what Peg was thinking about the most when she turned 21: Colin's father, William, who, tired of being Billy as a child (the whole 'Billy the Kid' thing), told everyone in college to call him Liam. That's where they met, at State, Peg with her liberal arts curriculum and Liam studying small business management (because he wanted to own a gas station). The next step for them would be marriage, then a family, then… well, things don't always work out, do they?

Peg smiled at Colin, "Believe you me, once I stopped coming here, I never would have thought that it would be my little boy to get me to come back."

Colin didn't like to think of himself as a little boy anymore. Isn't that the point of going to the Saloon in the first place. "What should we order?"

"Anything you'd like. This is a celebration, isn't it?"

"Champagne?"

Peg laughed. "Oh, don't be silly, I'm sure this Tongue character doesn't stock champagne in this place. This is where you go for a beer and a shot of rye."

"I was kidding, you know."

Peg looked over at the bar to see what beers were on tap, wondering if she'd ever know for sure when her son was kidding.

Colin had always been curious about that time in their lives, after his father died, and his mother was alone in a new town with a brand-new baby. Did she ever date anyone? Who were the friends she went out with? How did she ever manage to keep the gas station running while raising a kid as a single mom?

"Did you used to come here for a beer and a shot of rye?" he asked her.

With a wink, Peg confided, "A beer for sure. But no, I was never one for shots."

"Can I ask you why you used to come here?"

Peg laughed, "Why do you want to know? Did you feel

neglected?"

Colin felt sheepish, embarrassed by his curiosity. "I don't know. Was I?"

"I don't think so, honey." Peg reached across the table and quickly took Colin's hand before he could react. "Not for a minute. And what are you complaining about? Look how great you turned out."

Colin slipped his hand out of his mother's nonchalantly and leaned back in his chair. "I'm just a college grad, Mom, like five million other kids that graduated in May. Except they probably all got jobs this summer."

"That's not true and you know it. Besides, it wasn't meant to be. Graduate school. That's your ticket. You get one of those fancy MBAs, then you'll work anywhere you want."

"We'll see."

"What do you mean 'we'll see'?"

The waitress came over, apologizing for the delay. She'd been filling the order for the table of 10 who were sitting on the other side of the Saloon's main room.

The waitress was wearing jeans the way they were meant to be worn when it's a woman wearing them, and a Tongues Saloon t-shirt that had the sleeves and collar cut away. Under the tee, she wore a tight black long-sleeve top, which, without allowing a hint of cleavage, confirmed a perfectly proportioned chest for a slender gal of her 5'6" stature.

Peg thought she was cute, and a fine match for her boy, but she's clearly local, and he needed to be moving on. Grad school. Out of state.

Colin thought the waitress was hot and wondered how come he'd never seen her anywhere before.

"Sorry about the wait. Looks like a busy night. My name is Marilu. I know you, you're Peg, right? You own the gas station."

"That's right. You've been by?"

Marilu threw her weight to her left hip and Colin's

heart skipped. "Sometimes. I live down by Brookland. I usually gas up down there. No offense or nothing, it's just easier."

Peg smiled. "Oh, I understand. But you drive 30 minutes just to work here? I mean, no offense, but a pretty thing like you…"

Colin coughed.

"Oh, I'm sorry, this is my son, Colin."

"Your son?"

Peg laughed, "Well, you didn't think I was a cougar now, did you?"

Marilu blushed. "No, no, no. I just didn't know… I've never seen Colin at the gas station. How do you do?" Marilu gave Colin the full look, allowing him to take her in as well.

Despite himself, Colin spoke up, "I've been away at school."

"State?"

Colin sat up a little. "No. CU."

"Nice." Marilu threw her weight onto her right hip. "I went to State, graduated last year."

Colin sighed. "No jobs, right?"

"What do you mean? I work here." Marilu stared at him.

"No, I mean, you… I haven't been able to find a job, so I'm going to go get an MBA."

"Nice." Marilu smiled.

Peg saw her opportunity. "He leaves Monday. For graduate school. So tonight, we're celebrating."

Marilu moved her smile to Peg. "Nice. So, what can I get you?"

They ordered two pints of draft beer, but Colin was quickly losing his appetite for his long imagined first beer in Tongues. It was bad enough being here with his mother – to whom he was totally devoted, but that didn't make her a drinking buddy – and the idea that the first waitress to bring him a cold beer was a hottie more interested in small talk with his mom than with him did not bode well for how he always imagined a night in Tongues would play out.

When Marilu had gone, Peg tried to get Colin to relax. He had that telltale brow pucker above his nose. "I'm sure you'll meet plenty of cute girls in graduate school."

Colin leaned in with a softer voice. "Why do you keep going on about 'graduate' school? It's not that special."

Peg suppressed all the obvious comebacks. She didn't want to be his mom tonight. But she couldn't help herself, she would always be mom. "You can make anything special."

Colin quickly responded with another of Peg's oft-repeated bromides, "Nothing is special without you."

Peg smiled in appreciation, then they both harmonized on, "Everything can be special if you want it to be."

They laughed.

Marilu delivered their drinks with a quick, "Here you go, enjoy," not wanting to intrude on the shared laugh between mother and son.

"Cheers!" Colin raised his glass quickly and took a sip. He didn't want to risk Peg making a long maybe emotional toast about him moving so far away to go to 'graduate school.' "So, what's your milestone?"

"Mine? Oh, don't you know? I haven't been in here in 12 years, when the lady who owned the Saloon flipped her lid and stopped selling booze."

"Right, you must have told me that. What was her problem?"

"Jesus probably."

Colin choked a little on his sip of beer. "Meaning?"

"She got religion and decided that alcohol was a sin."

"Seems to me there's a lot of wine in the Bible."

"That's true. But they had to drink something. Keep in mind, they didn't have chocolate milk, flavored water or Coca Cola."

"Or beer," Colin offered.

"At least not that we know of. Peter always struck me as a beer guy, though."

"I see your point. Do you really want to build your church on a guy who cares about the bouquet of his beverage or whether it has good legs?"

Peg laughed, and Colin joined in, thinking 'Maybe this is going to be fun after all.'

Peg wondered just how much she'd miss her son's company. She took a mouthful of cold beer and thought, 'Now's the right time for him to go away. If he were around on weekend nights, neither of us could take the next step.' She asked him, "How do you like your first beer?"

"It's not my first beer, Mom. I hope that doesn't shock you. It's my first beer in Tongues. Since everyone in town knows Gasoline Peggy, there's no way I could drink in here until I turned 21."

Peg screwed up her face in disappointment. But not because her only child just confessed to under-age drinking. "People don't call me that still, do they?"

"Why not? You've been running the only gas station in town for... what? Twenty-two years?"

Peg put her glass down and let out a big sigh. "Close your eyes for a minute."

"Why?" Colin didn't know where this was going.

"Because I said so."

"Why?"

"Because I'm your mother."

He smiled at her. "Don't you have any other card to play?"

"Just close your eyes." Her tone was polite but firm.

"Fine." Colin took a sip a beer and agreed to play along.

Peg cleared her throat. "Okay. Now picture in your mind's eye the following made-up characters. Banker Bob."

"Who?"

"It's a make-believe character. Just humor me. Banker Bob. What's he look like?"

Eyes still closed, Colin responded, "Short guy, round, pinstripe suit, necktie too short. Round happy face, bit of a comb-over. Meaty handshake."

"Sounds more like Butcher Bob." They laughed.

Colin opened his eyes and explained, "He was a butcher, but the bank foreclosed on his shop, so he swore revenge and reinvented himself as a banker and embezzled millions."

Peggy smiled at her son. "Fine. Close your eyes. Next: Sheriff Joe."

With eyes closed, Colin offered, "Big hat, handlebar moustache. Bad teeth. Kind of wiry."

"Boy, you've got a strange imagination."

"Is there more? I'm getting thirsty." He was polite but wondering if he looked like an idiot talking to his mother in a bar with his eyes closed.

"Last one. Gasoline Peggy."

Colin hesitated. Now that he understood what the game was all about, he considered how to play it. Comedy? Because, drinking or otherwise, they were buddies. Or complimentary? After all, she's his mom, and an attractive 46-year-old widow who still gave a damn about looking pretty. "Wow, that's a tough one. There aren't that many English words that can describe a woman like that."

"Give it the ol' college try."

"Gasoline Peggy is a fatty boom-ba-latty, to put it politely."

"So, you're not going with English then."

"Can't do it."

"Go on."

"It's not her girth that's off-putting."

"So, she's off-putting?"

Colin opened his eyes and leaned forward, whispering in confidence, "Well, the word would be odorific. She's got a smell about her."

"A smell."

"From the gasoline," explained Colin.

"I see."

"But that's to be expected."

"Naturally."

"What makes her, well, unique, is the black hairy mole at the end of her nose, directly above the only tooth left in her head." Colin twisted his upper lip to model an ugly-looking smile.

"Is her nose in the middle of her face?" asked Peg.

"Most days."

"So, her only tooth is in the middle of her face as well."

"Exactly. Like a narwhal."

"Well, I don't think you're being fair to the narwhal."

Colin sat back and got serious. "Or to you. I get your point, Mom." He raised his glass. "I promise you this, Peg o My Heart, on this my 21ˢᵗ birthday week, as your only known offspring –"

"Cute."

" – I'll never again refer to you as Gasoline Peggy. And should any man, woman or child ever use that despicable moniker in reference to my dear old mom –"

"Careful now."

"– My dear *youngish* mom, I'll clobber 'em."

"Thank you, honey. That was almost sweet of you."

They clinked glasses and finished off their beers.

Marilu was suddenly back at their table. "Seems like a lot of toasting going on over here. Care for another round?"

Peg beamed, "Yes, please. We haven't even begun to toast."

About an hour later, Peg and Colin finished off a plate of chicken wings – one of the few items on the Saloon's 'Bar Eats' menu. Marilu came over and cleared their plates, asking, "How about another round?"

"Oh, not for me, thank you. But I would enjoy a cup

of decaf, please." Peg was feeling tired. Saturdays were always busiest at the gas station, with the highest volume of cars stopping in for gas, plus it was the day that most work came in for repairs. Over the years, Peg had hired a series of mechanics, never more than one at a time – there being only one bay in the garage. But when she did have a 'Mechanic on Duty' sign at the station, she enjoyed the extra income from a steady stream of customers, who needed more than a full tank of gasoline. She was often surprised that people from nearly an hour away would travel to Babel to have their cars worked on at her humble gas station, especially since no mechanic ever lasted more than three years there. So apparently it wasn't the men she hired that drew in the customers.

There had been seven mechanics at her A-1 Gas Station, not including Peg's husband Liam, who had turned his passion for cars and a keen entrepreneurial spirit into a short-lived dream of running his own gas station. There were plenty of stretches during the past 22 years when Peg didn't have a mechanic on duty, but she made do. Although a few came to Babel and left for the same reason (simple wanderlust), the others all eventually left because they couldn't square working for a woman who knew as much – maybe more – than they did about cars.

Peg was never mean about it or condescending. In fact, she tried to be helpful and instructive, sort of a mentor, which could be difficult when the mentee is an older man doing "a man's job." She liked everyone she hired. She just wanted them all to be good at their job, and honest, of course.

Peg was the only child of a racing car fanatic, Ralph Rooney, who, frankly, really wanted a son, and simply never accepted society's perspective that daughters should be raised like anything other than sons. So young Peggy, despite being the prettiest girl in school, became a darn good athlete and the only girl in shop class – one who would argue with her teacher about doing something better, the way her Dad taught her.

Ralph – who called himself Rocket, so most of his friends did too – would take Peggy to racing car events on hot summer weekends once she turned seven. Didn't matter if it were stock cars, dragsters, monster trucks or even demolition derbies, Rocket would go see anything anywhere within a three-hour drive of their home in Greater Curve. Bringing Peggy along ensured acquiescence from his wife, Lorelei, because it was 'bonding time' with his daughter. Lorelei herself wouldn't be caught dead watching cars race around a track or some such thing. Besides, she especially enjoyed Saturdays to herself, when she'd get pampered at the local salon. She knew who her daughter got her natural good looks from, and Lorelei wanted to ensure that she could still hold her own, despite being in her 30's.

When Rocket would take Peggy to the races, they'd get to visit with various racing teams because he was friendly with a few of the drivers and mechanics on the circuit. Mostly, he knew them from being a fan, but some were also customers. Rocket was one of the local FedEx drivers and his territory ranged for some 100 square miles and included Babel. Nothing excited him more than delivering engine parts that had been shipped overnight to some nearby semi-pro racer. On those days, Rocket would often get nailed for speeding, but the tickets were typically waived because of Rocket's father being a one-time county sheriff.

This rich history of "cars in her blood" – plus her fine looks – made Peg the "girl of my dreams" for her husband Liam. Naturally, she was pretty excited herself to fall for a boy who wanted to own his own gas station and repair shop. Their romance lasted through college, their wedding (one month after graduation), the opening of the A-1 Gas Station in Babel, the birth of their son Colin (named after Peg's sheriff grandfather) and abruptly ended the day Peg's husband was killed. It's not that she didn't love him anymore – she always would. But there's no romance in an empty bed when you're a 25-year widow with a newborn baby boy to raise and a gas station to run.

Looking into the eyes of that baby boy all grown up and drinking a beer with his Mom on the Saturday of Labor Day weekend, Peg started to get misty-eyed for the first time in years.

"I hope I did right by you, Colin, I hope I did."

"What are you talking about?"

"Tell me I was a good mother."

"You were a great... you *are* a great mother."

Colin was suddenly afraid she might start crying. The only thing he could imagine worse than being in a bar for your first legitimate beer with your own mother was to be in a bar for your first legitimate beer with your own mother, who – for God knows why – starts crying her eyes out.

Maybe she's sad he's leaving, maybe she's sad he's 21, maybe she's sad she's old, maybe she's sad she's a widow. Maybe beer makes widows with 21-year-old sons leaving for graduate school sad.

Whatever it was, Colin had to prevent it from happening. The crying. So he went for levity, again.

"What's the matter? You're not going to ask me to pay for my own beer, are you? That's it, isn't it? You left your girlie purse at home, under your crocheting, next to the dead cat you forgot to feed, and now you're asking your only son to cough up some scratch to pay for his own birthday booze. Nice job, Mom. Yeah, Mom of The Year, right here, folks. Right here." Colin bravely looked around, acting as if he was trying to draw everyone's attention, but, of course, hoping to attract none. He was pleased to see that neither the bartender, the two old guys at the bar, the table of 10, the hottie waitress, nor anyone else seemed to care.

Peg smiled. She knew what he was doing. Out of

respect for him, she wouldn't reach up and dab the corner of her eye, where a single teardrop was swelling in volume. She knew that gravity would eventually win out, and it would fall. But come what may, it falls, it falls. But she would not dab it away. She knew her son would be mortified if someone in the Saloon saw ol' Gasoline Peggy crying in her beer with her only begotten child.

So. She puffed up her cheeks and blew out a stream of sadness like a broken radiator.

"What was that?" Colin cringed.

Just then Marilu appeared with Peg's coffee. "Here you go. Anything for you... Colin, was it?"

"Yeah, no. Thanks. I'm good. Thanks." Once Marilu walked away, Colin asked again, "What was that face and sound?"

"Imagine I was blowing out the candle on your imaginary birthday cake."

"Okay." Again, Colin felt his mother's mood was fragile. "But that means you stole my wish."

"Oh, I wish I could," said Peg.

"And what would you wish for? That some knight in shining armor would ride into Babel on a mighty stead and sweep you away to a far-off kingdom?"

Peg smiled at Colin. "Really? Don't you know me at all?"

"Sorry. Replace the stead with a mustang. A '66 Mustang. Convertible, fire engine red."

Peg reached across the table and, avoiding both coffee cup and glass of beer, took Colin's hand.

Colin thought, 'Good God, she's holding my hand again.'

"Son," Peg started. "Happiness isn't about running away. Success isn't about being in another place. You can be successful, and happy, just standing in one spot."

"Okay." Colin expected there to be more. And there was.

"But," Peg continued. "It's okay to leave, too. It's just

that you can't pick a plant from one spot and lay it down somewhere else and think it's going to flower. You have to pull it up by the roots."

Colin interrupted. "Isn't that destroying the plant?"

"No. You're not killing the plant. You're not changing it. You're *trans*-planting it. It can still flower. But it needs its roots."

"With it," said Colin.

"Right."

"But then they're not roots."

Peg disregarded his challenge. "Roots are what you take with you."

Colin took a mouthful of beer and considered his mother. What to do about her? Worry? Worship? Or simply admire? "Okay, so why didn't you move and take your roots with you? Once Dad..."

Peg cut him off. "It's a fair question, and I'd be lying if I didn't admit to wondering about that so many times... so, so many times, you have no idea. But what it came down to was this: your Dad made a really smart deal on setting up the gas station, buying the real estate and all. I've always enjoyed the business. And sure, I was plenty lonely at times, but I had my baby boy to keep me company. I only regretted you not having a Dad."

Colin smiled, "I think I turned out just fine with only a mom. Because she's a great one." He tapped his beer glass to her coffee cup.

"Don't do what I did, Colin, because I did it. Make your own decision, make your own way. Don't worry about me. You go away to graduate school and find yourself."

Colin cocked his head at Peg the way a dog does to remind you that it doesn't understand English.

"I'll make you a deal, Colin. Find yourself, then I'll come find you."

"You'd leave the gas station? You'd leave Babel?"

"Yep. Roots and all."

At that moment, Marilu swept by again and asked if they needed anything else. It was Colin who responded, "No, thank you. I think it's time to go."

Tongue's Tale 3

The only time I was in a fistfight was when I was 14. I didn't want to fight, but it was the honorable thing to do. The school bully was picking on a little kid, and I intervened. Thought I could talk some sense into this guy, who was much bigger than me. I didn't think I was being brave, I remember being really nervous. So, I just started talking and talking and talking, trying my hardest to be persuasive, I guess. But I guess I was just annoying. So, the bully says, "Will you shut up!" and with that, he lets fly with a vicious upper cut. I was still talking so my tongue happened to get caught between my teeth. Cut the tip right off. Blood everywhere. Best part... well, actually, the only good part of the story: All the blood made the bully faint. He was never a bully after that. People thought I was a hero. But I learned my lesson: don't talk so much.

MOON ROCKS (8:30 PM)

Gus got to the front door of the Saloon first, but when he turned around to say something to Dom, he saw that a woman and a college-age boy had fallen in step behind them. Without fanfare, Gus held the door open for them and gave the woman a smile and nod. She smiled back.

The kid said, "Thanks," and Gus gave him a nod, too, but wiped the smile from his face. They locked eyes for a moment, with Gus' expression saying, 'Don't worry, I wasn't smiling at your mom.'

After they passed, Dom headed through the door, but Gus grabbed him and gave him an arched eyebrow look that clearly conveyed 'Wait.'

When the woman and son were out of earshot, Gus asked, "You know who that is?"

"Looks like the lady owns the gas station."

"S'right. Gasoline Peggy. Man, she's still a looker."

Gus released Dom and they headed in, Dom falling in step behind Gus. As Gus had lived in Babel for nearly 40 years and Dom fewer than four months, Dom deferred to his friend in many ways. As they bellied up to the bar, Dom asked, "She single?"

"Widow. That's her boy. All growed up, as they say."

"What happened to the dad?"

Gus looked at Dom, feigning disappointment. He liked having the upper hand with his new neighbor. Dom had moved into the house next to Gus', over Memorial Day weekend. A summer of friendly barbecues revealed how much the two had in common. Married, kids in grade

35

school, each a boy and a girl. Dogs, who also got along. Wives as well. Gus was an electrician, and Dom ran his own commercial print shop.

Gus ordered two scotches from the bartender – whom he insisted on calling Tom, despite everyone in town calling him Tongue, and the establishment being named 'Tongues Saloon.' Gus was simply put off by the nickname. The bartender was friendly enough that he didn't seem to mind Gus calling him Tom.

Realizing Dom wouldn't have known about Gasoline Peggy's husband, Gus said, "Don't you know anything?"

"Only what you tell me."

The bartender placed two rocks glasses in front of the men, atop Tongues Saloon coasters. "Gentlemen, start your engines."

"Thanks, Tom."

"Thanks. Tongue." Dom winked at Gus.

Gus shot Dom a look. "Drink up wise-acre and remember, you're buying. Now let me tell you the tale about the husband."

"I'm all ears." Dom toasted his friend, but accidentally spilt a splash of scotch over the rim of the glass.

Gus looked at him. "And thumbs."

"Hunh?"

"Never mind. Listen up. Something like twenty years ago it must have been, Peggy and her husband, his name was William…"

"Bill or Billy?" asked Dom.

"Actually, he called himself Liam."

"I never like Williams. Can't trust them the way you can trust a Bill or Billy."

"What about Jack?"

Dom was confused. "Jack who?"

"Jack-ass. Stop being one and listen up."

Dom laughed.

"So, they buy the old Harrison's gas station and fix it up. Pour good money into it. Paid off in the long run, though. Place must be a gold mine. Anyway, the husband got killed."

"You don't say."

"I do say. In fact, I just said it. Why do people say 'you don't say' when someone just said something? Drives me nuts."

Dom offered his insight. "People say things all the time, don't make any sense, but doesn't keep them from saying it."

"You can say that again."

Dom stared at Gus. "Are you giving me an example, or did you want me to repeat myself?"

"Funny. Still writing your own material?"

The men laughed and enjoyed more of their scotches.

Dom chimed back in, "That reminds me, I saw a comedian on the television the other night. Had a whole thing about the letter B and how it's silent in the word 'subtle.'"

"Really. Must have been fascinating."

"No, really. Funny stuff, you would have liked it."

"Dumb," Gus said.

"Alright, you don't have to be mean. I thought it was a funny routine. Guess you had to be there."

Gus lightly slapped Dom's arm with the back of his hand. "Don't be so sensitive. I was giving you another example."

"Example of what?"

"Silent B. Dumb."

"Oh yeah. Good one. Can you think of any others?"

"Yeah. Dumber and dumbest."

Dom assessed his friend for a moment, but then had a eureka. "Dumbbell's an interesting one. Two B's. One silent, one not."

"Kinda like us." Gus smiled broadly. "Think about that one while you work on that drink."

The bartender, Tongue, came over and asked, "Two more, gentlemen?"

"Sounds right to me," answered Dom.

Gus consented with a slight nod. "Tom, tell Dumb here... sorry, I meant Dom. Tell him how you lost your tongue?"

With a big smile, Tongue answered, "I didn't lose it. I just forgot where I put it down. I'm sure it's here someplace. Maybe I dropped it in a martini, instead of an olive." He winked at Gus.

"Please!" Gus feigned disgust. "I'll lose my appetite."

Tongue leaned in. "Wanna lose your appetite? Let me tell you about the time I was licking the lid from a can of cream of mushroom soup, when an earthquake shook my hand so hard, I cut off the tip of my tongue." Tongue started to laugh heartily, egging Gus to join him.

Dom spoke up. "I like the one about you daring the ranch-hand to knock a caterpillar off your tongue with a bullwhip."

Tongue coughed out a little laugh, privately pleased with himself. He backed away along the bar to pour fresh scotches. He called out, "Dagnabbit Dom, I never said any such thing. My earthquake story, now that's the truth."

Dom said to Gus, "He is a funny guy."

"Yeah, and subtle, too."

The men lifted their glasses to finish off their first drinks.

Wiping his mouth with the back of his hand, Dom announced, "I got a question."

"I'm sure you do."

"Why is a drink from Scotland called a scotch but a man from Scotland is called a Scotsman?"

Gus countered. "Oh yeah, well, let me ask you this one. If a man from Scotland who drank Scotch, was named Scott, spelled with two Ts, why is he a Scot spelled with one T?"

"He's not. He's Scottish, with two Ts."

Gus conceded, "Good one. For a minute there, I

thought I got off scot-free."

They laughed and clinked glasses again.

"Psst." An unexpected voice suddenly got the attention of both Gus and Dom. They looked to their right, past a few empty bar stools, to an old man, whom Gus had seen perched in the same spot at the end of the bar plenty of times before. Next to him was a younger man, whom Gus recognized as the owner of the local hardware store.

In an exaggerated stage whisper, the old man said to Gus and Dom, "Drambuie is from Scotland."

At that moment, Tongue placed two fresh drinks in front of Gus and Dom, noting loudly for all to hear, "But not Jim Bowie. He was from Kentucky."

Gus and Dom were totally dumbfounded. Still, Gus raised his new glass of scotch and toasted the old-timer, in a poor attempt at a Scottish brogue. "To yer 'ealth, lad."

The old man didn't respond, just turned his attention back to his hardware store companion.

Dom looked at Tongue and Gus and shrugged. He was curious about the random exchange, but he didn't care enough to ask for clarification. Instead, he leaned over and poked Gus in the arm with his index finger. "Knish."

Tongue took that as a cue to move on. "Cheers, gentlemen."

"What in the world is a ka-nish?"

"A knish, my friend, is an urban delicacy sold, once upon a time, by street vendors selling hot dogs. Nowadays, you're lucky if you can find them in a delicatessen."

Gus smirked at Dom. "You're not really telling me what it is, now are you?"

"Think of it as a mashed potato burger, but instead of a bun, the potato, made with onions, has fried dough sealing it, like an envelope."

"And this would be something you'd eat?"

"Oh yeah. Hot. But first you slice it open and spread

in some mustard." Dom closed his eyes to savor the image. "Delicious."

"Maybe. Sounds interesting, I guess," Gus conceded. "But my real guess is you ain't finding no ka-nish in these parts."

"These parts. That's a funny expression, too. Like it's random parts of a chicken or something."

Gus squinted at him. "Okay, I don't think you'll find a knish in this part of the country."

"Wish I knew that before I moved to Babel."

Gus smiled at his friend, "Before you moved to Babel, you probably wish you knew that no one moves to Babel. They only move away."

Dom waved his glass. "I wouldn't have come if I knew there were no knishes."

Gus looked away. "You're not waiting for me to say something like, I'm happy you decided to come to Babel or something like that, are you? Because this ain't no Lifetime movie or Hallmark card."

"Not at all, Gus. I'm waiting for you to ask me why I said 'knish' in the first place."

"Getting crafty, aincha? Okay, Dominic, how come you said, 'ka-nish' in the first place?"

"How come it's pronounced ka-nish, and not 'nish,' like knife. Knife has a silent K. Or knit, or knowledge, or knack. So how come 'nish' gets the 'ka'?"

Gus took a long sip of scotch and thought over his response. "Let me say this about that. First off, having no prior knowledge of a knish, I don't really have a knack for answering you, so I'll just stick to my knitting and say that there are some things in life that are just useless. Like the K in knife."

Dom smiled at his friend, always amused at his less-than-subtle comic turns. "Well done, Constantine, well done. Cheers." Dom offered up his glass.

Pleased with himself, Gus accepted the tribute and clinked glasses with Dom, "Cheers."

After his sip, Dom swirled the ice cubes in his glass. "I have another question for you."

"Oh good. For a minute there I thought we'd die of embarrassment in a prolonged awkward silence."

Dom held up his glass. "Rocks. Why 'rocks'? Rocks don't make liquids colder. Rocks don't melt. Ice cubes. Ice. Cubes. Why not just 'cubes.' 'I'll have a scotch and cubes, please.' Or 'Scotch on ice.' I don't get it. Why 'rocks'?"

"You know, if you freeze a rock, you can use it instead of an ice cube, and it won't melt and dilute your scotch. A glass of frozen rocks is actually better than ice when you're drinking scotch."

Dom considered this. "But you can't really freeze a rock, can you? Besides, wouldn't it make your drink dirty and crunchy?"

"I think you'd wash the rocks really well before you freeze them."

"Okay, but you could still break your teeth drinking a drink with rocks."

Gus pondered another retort. "Maybe they should serve scotch in a thermos. This way the scotch stays cold, and you don't have to worry about ice diluting your drink. Or rocks breaking your teeth." He drank up.

"I like that idea. The thermos was the best thing ever invented. Keeps cold things cold, hot things hot. Simple and brilliant. I wonder who invented the thermos."

Gus responded with great self-assurance, "NASA."

"No way."

"Sure way. It's not like they took a refrigerator and stove with them to the moon. They needed a way to keep things at a constant temperature. So they invented thermos technology."

Dom looked at Gus, trying to decipher whether or not he was pulling his leg. He didn't consider himself gullible, yet he knew his neighbor could occasionally weave a tall tale when the mood hit him.

"I don't mean to eavesdrop, gentlemen." It was Tongue, acting all sheepish as he ran a wet rag along the bar top, wiping away not much of anything. "I heard you talking about the mighty thermos and drinking scotch from it. Well, I think you might be interested to know two true facts."

Gus and Dom were hooked, and they leaned in for some knowledge.

Tongue spoke confidently, but without a trace of bragging, "The thermos was invented by James Dewar. Yes, he was a Scotsman. But, he was not related to his fellow Scotsman John Dewar, who created the Scotch whiskey that bears his name." Tongue just beamed. "Now what do you think about that?"

Gus and Dom looked at each other and their expressions quietly confirmed that neither believed the bartender. Not wanting to tick him off though, Gus toasted Tongue, saying, "To your subtle knowledge on the subject then, I raise my scotch to you."

That made Tongue laugh and succeeded in moving him back down the bar.

Gus looked at Dom, who just shrugged. Dom mentally reached back and picked up the thread of their conversation – the truth they knew. "You know, you think about all that technology that did go into sending Man to the moon and look what they come back with. Rocks."

Gus laughed. "Moon rocks. What a useless souvenir."

Dom wondered, "You know what they did with them?"

"Probably stuck 'em in a museum or in some government lab where no one could touch 'em or see 'em."

Dom egged him on, "Yeah, but you know what they could do with them moon rocks?"

"What?"

"Well, think about how cold the moon is. The astronauts probably used the rocks to chill their scotches."

Gus smiled, he got the joke. "Pretty expensive ice cubes. Billions of dollars. Sure could buy a lot thermoses for that."

Dom looked away and said to himself. "Thermi."

Gus asked, "How's that?"

Dom finished his second drink and looked back at Gus. "You want another?"

"What? A ka-nish? I haven't had even one yet."

"No, a Scottish scotch made by a Scotsman named Scottie."

"Nah. I promised the wife I wouldn't keep you out late. She doesn't want you getting in trouble again. Pay the man, Dom, and we'll be on our way."

"You're a wise man, Gus, a wise man."

Dom paid the tab, shared friendly 'good nights' with the bartender, and fell in step behind Gus as they headed towards the front door. As Gus pulled it open, three women entered, giggling. They each thanked Gus and he smiled in return, saying, "Lookin' fine, ladies, lookin' fine." When they were out of earshot, Dom said to Gus, "Well, that wasn't very subtle."

"Sorry, Dom, just feelin' a little numb."

Tongue's Tale 4

One time I was watching the Olympics. Fencing. Great sport. Got real interested and signed up for classes. You know those silly looking masks they wear that look like mesh food strainers. Well, just remember that if you and your roommate are horsing around with real epees, mesh food strainers are not suitable substitutes for those silly looking masks.

GIRLFRIEND IS BETTER (9:30 PM)

Carl held the front door for Donna, as was his custom, because it was the way he was raised. Donna responded with the slightest hint of a curtsy because she thought Carl's manners were so cute and old-fashioned. Although she wasn't raised with good manners necessarily, she sure did appreciate them. When she came to Babel three years ago, settling in after college, she noticed that manners meant a lot in these parts. She often thought that her success in moving up to be a manager at the shoe store Well-Heeled was due to her passion for shoes, her innate fashion sense and her photographic memory of the inventory, but she made note that politeness at all times was a smart policy. Didn't matter if it was the boss, the stock boy or the grouchiest customer (who was usually Mrs. Eleanor Crabtree, as her name implied), Donna made a point of winning over people with her well-mannered smile.

Finding a similar politeness in Carl tickled Donna. She was so relieved to see that he had good people skills despite being the head of a call center out at the corporate park about an hour south of Babel. Okay, that wasn't being fair to Carl, his department or call center people in general. 'What I meant was,' Donna thought to herself, 'I like this boy.'

This was their fourth date in as many weeks, but it was the first time Carl had brought Donna to Tongues Saloon. It was his usual hangout, and he liked the owner. Carl thought Tongue was a good guy, and funny. (His real name was Tom, but he never used that). Tongue was missing the tip of his tongue – that alone made Carl laugh – and he always had a funny made-up story about how he lost it.

Carl had wrestled with taking Donna to what he considered "his spot" out of fear that if the new relationship didn't work out, well, sharing the Saloon in the future might be a problem.

But tonight, on the Saturday night of Labor Day weekend, he decided to bring his date to his spot after a movie, so they could get a couple of drinks, something to eat, and catch a little bit of the game. Carl wasn't big on going to the movies, he was more of a sports guy, and would rather spend the night in front of the TV watching any kind of game.

A recent epiphany – his mother reminded him that he'd be turning 30 in November and that he still wasn't married – convinced him that maybe he needed to change his attitude about what made for a good time on a date.

Once inside the Saloon, Carl directed Donna towards an empty table in the main bar area. It may have looked like a random choice to Donna, but Carl was precise in his selection, as well as which chairs they should sit in. He hoped to surreptitiously keep an eye on the two televisions behind the bar that were broadcasting different games. But the jig was up when Donna switched seats, saying, "Oh, let me sit next to you so I can watch the games, too."

At first he was embarrassed, but Carl quickly realized that sharing an interest in sports could be a good thing.

"So, what did you think of the movie?" Donna said.

This was not the kind of conversation Carl liked to have. "It was alright."

"Alright? Just alright? You didn't love it? I mean, I loved it. And if you didn't, that's okay. I was just hoping that you liked it some. I'm sorry you didn't like it."

"I didn't say I didn't like it. I thought it was alright." Carl smiled at Donna.

"Okay. But saying you thought it was alright is just a polite way of saying you didn't like it."

"No, it's not. It's saying that it was alright. Not great, but not bad either."

"Interesting. If I thought something was not great but not bad either, I'd say that that something is good. Don't you think?" Donna leaned in towards Carl.

"Good is alright."

"Exactly. So you liked the movie." Donna leaned back with a smile.

"Sure."

"What didn't you like about the movie?"

"I just said I liked the movie."

"I know. But, here's the thing. I loved the movie."

"That's good. I'm happy you loved the movie." Carl graciously gave Donna another smile.

"Do you want to know why I loved the movie?"

"Yes. I liked the movie enough, but I'd like to hear why you loved the movie."

Donna looked at Carl, wondering if he was poking fun at her. Coming from another man, Carl's sentence might have been sarcastic and perhaps even mean. But not from Carl, he's too polite. Donna didn't give it another moment's thought; she was too eager to talk about the movie. "It was so romantic."

"Funny how romantic comedies will do that," Carl said smiling. Concerned that Donna didn't smile back, he offered, "That was a joke."

"I know. I was just thinking about how you look like him."

"Who?"

"The guy in the movie."

"I don't look like…"

"No. Silly. I meant the guy who played the best friend, the guy who loses the girl because he's too obsessed with his music career."

"Oh yeah. Yeah? You think I look like that guy?"

47

"Don't you think?"

"I don't know. Maybe. I've been called worse."

"Ha! Like being called a movie star is a bad thing. What worse have you been called?"

Carl looked over at the bar and caught the eye of the waitress. She had just given a big order to Tongue, who always tended bar. She smiled and headed right over.

"Hi folks, how are you tonight? I'm Marilu."

Carl gave her an appreciative smile. Since this was his hangout, he obviously knew Marilu, and she knew him. But she didn't know Carl's date, so she played it safe. She liked Carl – he was polite and never hit on her, which was refreshing. For all she knew, the woman with him could be a sister or a co-worker or a whatever. Didn't matter to her, Marilu just didn't want to assume anything.

"Hi there. Can we see a menu, please?" asked Carl.

"Sure thing." Marilu reached into her back pocket for two menus. The food selection at Tongues was pretty limited. "Do you know what you'd like to drink?"

"I'll have a draft. Donna, do you know what you'd like?"

"How 'bout a good ol' gin and tonic?"

"How 'bout it! Sounds good ol' to me." Marilu winked at Donna.

"Lots of lime." Donna mashed her lips together as if imagining the tart taste already.

"That's how I like it, too. I'll be back with your drinks in just a minute, then see if you'd like to eat anything."

Once Marilu was out of earshot, Donna said, "She's nice. Very friendly. And polite."

"Yep. I've seen her in here before, but I never remember her name."

"Did she ever say you look like a movie star, or does she call you something worse?" Donna laughed and Carl joined in. As he glanced away, at the games no doubt, Donna looked over and assessed Marilu, who was leaning on the bar watching as Tongue filled a pitcher of beer and a carafe of white wine. Donna quipped, mostly to herself, "I bet she's a five. And a half."

Carl heard her but wasn't sure how to respond. There was no way he was going to get involved in a conversation with a woman about rating another woman – it could be a trap disguised as an innocent remark, inside a "fishing for a compliment" ruse. Plus he had no idea what kind of scale Donna was using or whether a 5½ was good or bad or just alright. He played it safe with a distracted, "Hunh?"

Donna looked at him, almost sympathetically. How could he be expected to know? "Her shoe size."

"That mean she has big feet?" Because of Donna's blank, silent stare, Carl added, "No, I guess not. You really know your shoes, don'cha? Must be hard to leave work at work, when everywhere you look you see shoes. Even watching the game." Carl pointed a thumb towards the TV, thinking, 'Maybe we can talk sports now.'

Donna smiled, "But it's my passion. I just love it. I don't care if it's sneakers or stilettos, pumps or cleats, if it goes on your feet, I'm interested."

Carl got an interesting idea, and slowly leaned over to Donna, putting his face very close to hers. She didn't know if he was going to kiss her or scare her. At the very last moment, he diverted his face towards her ear. He whispered, "How do you feel about... socks?"

Donna burst out laughing and Carl joined in with a big smile, proud that he gave her such a belly laugh.

In return she gave him a weak punch on the arm, "Oh Carl, I thought you were going to bite me or something. That's too funny. Socks. You kidder."

Carl leaned back feeling quite full of himself, "You know, I stole that move from the guy in the movie."

"Hunh?"

"Remember when the guy – you know, the guy you claim I look like, the loser friend – when he goes up to the blonde with the... you know, the one who took off her... before she jumped. Anyway the guy goes in to kiss her, well that's what she thinks, right? And instead, he says to her, in that bad fake accent..." Carl deepened his voice and came out with an oddly European tone... 'I used to pay for the sex and violence.'"

Donna again hit him with a blank, silent stare, and he moved his arm away expecting to be hit by another punch as well. "What?" asked Carl defensively.

"That's not what he said. He said, 'I used to play alto sax and violin.'"

"No way," Carl said, getting a little red in the face.

"Trust me. Way."

Carl noodled this over, realizing pretty quickly that he must be wrong. What Donna heard made a lot more sense, considering the guy in the movie was a musician trying to recover the talents he had abandoned in order to travel the world seeking the meaning of life.

"Okay, I'll buy that. My bad, as they say."

Donna smiled away his foolishness. "So, what did you think of the movie?"

Carl felt squeamish, thinking, 'Really? Didn't I already lose this game?'

Marilu was suddenly at their table, placing down their drinks: a frothy cold beer and a gin and tonic with lots of lime. "Sorry for the delay, folks. That big table over there, they're a thirsty bunch. Oh, by the way, Tongue..." Marilu looked at Donna, "He's the bartender." She looked back at Carl, "Tongue wanted me to say, 'First round's on him, Mr. Fever.' That's exactly what he wanted me to say."

She smiled and walked away. Carl stared at her ass as she walked away -- not out of any kind of lechery – he just didn't know where else to look, because he sure didn't want to look at Donna. He could feel Donna staring at him. He could sense her mouth slightly agape, her head tilting just a smidge, as she tried to digest what she had just heard.

Carl took a deep breath. He had known this moment

would come. In fact, he'd been planning it. Maybe not for tonight. But he knew he'd get there. He sure hoped to. Since their first date he knew that if he was going to get anywhere with Donna, where he did want to get to, he'd have to face up to this moment. And thinking about it now, wouldn't it be better to have the conversation in a bar than in the bedroom, where, if things went south, it would be horribly awkward? At least here, sitting in Tongues, it seemed safer.

Emboldened by this logic and a fair dose of hope, Carl picked up his beer and offered a salute towards Donna, "Cheers."

"Cheers to you, Mr. Fever." Donna smiled. "Looks like maybe you have a secret. Anything you'd like to get off your chest?"

"Funny you should say that."

They sipped their drinks and eyed each other patiently. Donna was feeling curious but also guarded. She was very happy with how her relationship with Carl had been progressing. She worried that something was about to change that.

Carl wanted to feel he had nothing to lose, but the reality was that he stood to lose Donna. However, he had no choice. There wasn't much you could do when the truth was written in indelible ink on your skin.

"So, I guess you're curious about why Tongue calls me Mr. Fever."

"I'm curious why he'd call you anything other than Carl."

"Well, I've been coming here long enough that we're friendly, I guess. Not really buddies, but he's a good guy."

"What do you call him?"

Carl looked at her, wondering if she was trying to trap him. "Tongue. I call him Tongue, everyone does." He leaned in to speak confidentially. "His real name is Thomas. But no one calls him Tom or Tommy. Just Tongue." He hoped that sharing this apparent secret would keep Donna friendly.

She sipped her gin and tonic and the limes made her squint. "So, should I call you Mr. Fever?"

Carl jumped in. "Okay, here's the story. Full disclosure. You'd find out sooner or later, and I was hoping you'd find out soon, just not necessarily like this. I have a tattoo on my chest."

Donna's eyes widened slightly. "A tattoo of what?"

"Nothing. Just words."

"What's it say?"

"Carlton Fever."

"Carlton Fever," Donna repeated it slowly to make sure she heard it right. "Who's that?"

"Me. Kinda."

"So, it just says Carlton Fever in big letters across your chest?"

"No, actually it's pretty small, and it's just over my heart."

Donna smiled, but she hid it from Carl by taking a longer sip of her drink.

Carl took the cue and hit his beer as well, wondering how this was going over with Donna.

"Can I see it?"

"Of course, you can. But not right now, if you don't mind. Unless you want me stripping off my shirt in the middle of the Saloon like I'm a Chippendale's dancer."

Donna laughed. "Well, I don't know. Do you have what it takes to be a stripper?"

Carl laughed nervously, and leaned in again to share another confidence, "All men think so, but not many of us do, do we?"

Donna threw her head back and laughed louder, "I think you're right." Carl realized she must be picturing something, or someone, to make her laugh that loud.

When she stopped, she got serious and asked, politely, "So what's the story behind 'Carlton Fever'?"

With a final gulp, Carl finished his pint. "Well,

Carlton's my full name, right?"

"Okay, I didn't know that. But I like it."

"And, once upon a time, I had a girlfriend. Okay, so she was more than a girlfriend. We lived together, and we were together all the time, and we were going to get married, I mean we were going to get engaged." The words raced out of Carl who had become suddenly quite nervous. "That was the plan anyway, get engaged, get married, the whole thing. She was like my whole life at the time. She meant everything."

Donna interrupted him. "Just say 'girlfriend.' It's better that way." She was patient because she knew this was important and she didn't want Carl to be nervous.

"Right. Girlfriend is better."

"What was her name?" asked Donna, politely.

Carl hesitated. He knew from experience, once you named something out loud, you gave it power. "Eve."

"Eve." Donna repeated it to show Carl that she understood. "And so?"

"So, I got a tattoo."

"I'm sorry. Connect the dots for me."

"The tattoo I got, over my heart said, 'Carl and Eve.'"

Again, Donna repeated his words, "'Carl and Eve.'"

"Yeah, but not the word 'and.' It was the letter N. Carl 'n' Eve. Like rock 'n' roll."

"Got it."

"Anyway, things didn't work out with Eve. Obviously. She's out of my life. Long time. Almost two years now." Carl looked at Donna. She didn't seem upset, but she clearly wasn't working it all out in her head. Carl would have to spell it out, literally.

"So last year, I went back to the tattoo parlor and had them fix my tattoo. All the guy could come up with was to make 'Carl N' into 'Carlton' by squeezing in the T and O. I'll admit that it doesn't look too good. Then he just added an F and an R to turn 'Eve' into 'Fever.' So now I got 'Carlton Fever' on my chest." He took a deep breath and let it out slowly. "I'm not proud of it, I'm not happy with it. But that's the truth."

Donna finished her drink. "Let's get another round, okay? But no snacks."

With tremendous relief, Carl looked for Marilu. She caught his eye as she was walking between tables putting down coasters. She called over to them, "Two more of the same?"

Donna answered, "Please," as Carl called back with an emphatic "Yes!"

They sat in silence until Marilu placed the fresh drinks in front of them.

Donna raised her glass, "Here's to you, Mr. Fever. Thank you for sharing your story. I appreciate you being open and honest with me."

They clinked glasses and drank.

Donna leaned in to speak confidentially. "Carl, I'd like to show you my tattoo. Later on. If you'd like."

Carl's eyes widened like saucers. "I'd like that, I'd like that a lot, Donna." He sat back and smiled, then leaned in again to conspire. "I always hoped I could share having a tattoo with, you know, my, my… what? I guess you're more than a date, right?"

"Say, girlfriend, Carl. It's better."

Tongue's Tale 5

When I was a kid, I got into this whole martial arts craze. Taking karate lessons, watching kung fu movies, buying all kinds of stupid things like nunchucks and shuriken, those metal stars that ninjas throw. One time I was in my bedroom just tossing this ninja star up in the air. Well I threw it too high and it stuck in the ceiling. I climbed on a chair to knock it down and just as I reached it, the star fell straight down and cut off the tip of my tongue. God's honest truth.

MAKING FLIPPY FLOPPY (9:15 PM)

On the Saturday of Labor Day weekend, Harrison's Suprette closed at 9:00 pm, an hour earlier than usual. It was a decision that the owner, George Garrison, had made a week earlier, and he made sure all his regular customers knew about the change. He had flyers printed up and left on each of the store's three cash register counters. He had a poster placed on both the entrance door as well as the exit door. He also announced, once an hour, all week long: "Attention shoppers. Please note that Harrison's Suprette will be closing at nine o'clock p.m. on this Saturday. Please shop early for the holiday weekend. Thank you."

George Garrison, who bought Harrison's Suprette 16 years ago, made many changes to upgrade, improve and expand the offerings of the store, but he had no interest in changing its name from Harrison's. He thought a name change, from Harrison's to Garrison's, would confuse customers; the coincidence of the names amused him.

What amused his employees was George's obsession of never wanting to confuse his customers. Garrison's Labor Day announcement became the latest source of merriment among his late crew, the six workers whose shift ran from 3:00 pm to 9:00 pm, weeknights and Sundays, 3:00 pm to 10:00 pm on Saturdays. Bette, Brenda and Delores were the three cashiers, who doubled as stockers; Lewis was the deli-man and butcher; Arthur was responsible for produce and maintenance; and Jimmy (now called Jim) was the night manager.

Jim Helper was George's nephew and heir apparent. The 24-year-old was the son of George's sister Alice. George had no children himself and had always been quite fond of young Jimmy, who started working in the supermarket as a stock boy at age 10, obviously off the books.

Jimmy rose through the ranks and worked in every department at every function. He went away to a two-year community college out of state that offered a curriculum in retail management. When he returned four years ago, it was clear to everyone that he would one day take over. Not because George treated him any differently, but because Jimmy now insisted that people call him 'Jim.'

Bette, Brenda and Delores, who had worked side-by-side with him for 14 years, found an amusing conceit in Jimmy, but not a mean one. To tease him, but in a respectful way, they began to call him Mr. Jim. Jim understood that they were teasing him, but he really liked the sound of it. So he tolerated the ribbing, and the ladies tolerated him trying to be intolerable.

Working at Harrison's Suprette was not the best paying job in Babel, but it wasn't very stressful. George kept a clean store with quality goods at fair prices. People liked to shop there, and his workers liked to work there. During the 16 years he ran the store, two other merchants tried to open supermarket style operations in town, but neither lasted three years. Babel was a one-horse town, if you consider a supermarket to be as valuable as a horse.

For the Saturday of Labor Day weekend, Bette struck upon a fun idea. Since they all had to work anyway, why not have a little party for the late shift? She proposed to Brenda and Delores at closing time on the Thursday prior, "We should all go out on Saturday. We got that extra hour off – with pay. Let's go to the Saloon for our own Labor Day party."

"Who?" Brenda asked.

"All of us night-owls. You, me, Delores, Lewis, Arthur,

and of course we'd ask Mr. Jim, too."

"Get out," said Delores. "Why'd we do that?"

"Fun, that's all. It'd be fun."

Brenda supported Bette, "Sure it would. I like it."

"No, I mean, why would we ask Mr. Jim?" Delores was eager to clarify her position.

"Why not?"

"He's the boss," explained Delores.

Brenda suggested, "Sounds like the right reason to include him."

Bette protested, "Oh, don't think of it like that. We invite him because it's the right thing to do."

So, the threesome agreed to go out after the store closed on Saturday, and they invited the three men they worked with, including Jim Helper. As it turned out, Lewis the butcher already had plans for a card game at his neighbor's house, and Arthur had promised his wife to take her to the 9:15 show at Babel's one-screen movie theater. Jim Helper, however, was delighted with the invitation. He dutifully reported it to his boss/uncle, noting, "I think this get-together is good for morale and a clear sign of my team's respect for my position." George was not impressed but told his nephew to have a good time. Jim pressed his luck a bit and asked George if he might be reimbursed – as a business expense – for buying a round of drinks for his employees. George politely turned him down, "I don't think that would be good for morale, Jim. What about the day shift? What about the next time someone wants to go out drinking? Am I to pay for all that, too?"

Jim was embarrassed that his uncle might think he was being cheap. He had hoped to look more important to three of their employees by saying the company was picking up the tab. Nonetheless, Jim went out to Tongues Saloon that Saturday genuinely interested in having a good time and showing his team that, as a good manager, he was well-rounded and had good interpersonal skills.

The ladies arrived first, as Jim stayed behind to lock up and set the store's alarms. Tongues Saloon was not an unfamiliar destination for any of the women, nor was it a regular haunt. On different occasions they had each swapped the stories told by that oddball bartender about how he had lost the tip of his tongue. Each of the ladies was somewhat grossed out by the name Tongues and referred to the establishment only as the Saloon. In fact, when the young waitress served them their drinks, Bette, Brenda and Delores flipped the coasters upside down, so they wouldn't have to look at the Saloon's vulgar logo of smiling lips and a chopped off tongue.

When Jim arrived, his employees were seated at a square table for four, smack-dab in the middle of the bar. Brenda felt self-conscious being out in the open where everyone could watch, and she thought it a little awkward for these three middle-aged "women of color" to be waiting for their white boss – a man half their age. Delores pouted like she still had a chip on her shoulder about inviting Mr. Jim. But Bette lit up and flashed a dazzling smile to greet him. "Here we are, Mr. Helper, right here."

Jim smiled to himself, since there was no way he could have missed them in the Saloon, which boasted fewer than twenty patrons in its oversized main room, the heart of the roadhouse. Jim was quite familiar with the Saloon and had spent many nights playing pool and darts in the back room, often with guys he went to high school with, but plenty of times with strangers – usually truckers – who were just passing through. He was good enough at both games to hold his own against all comers, but he'd never play for money. Maybe a beer or a shot, but never for money. On one hand he didn't want the hard feelings about money to overshadow the sportsmanship of competition, and on the other hand, he lived too hand-to-mouth to afford to lose money gambling on bar sports.

"Good evening, team. It's been so long since I've seen

y'all."

Delores wasn't shy about rolling her eyes at Jim's playful tone as he tried to ingratiate himself with his employees.

Bette waved him into the empty chair between her and Delores, and across from Brenda. She worked this out ahead of time. It meant that he'd be looking at Brenda most of the time – but that was okay, Bette was confident she was still the prettiest of the three, although they all worked hard to stay as attractive as three working single moms could be. She knew Mr. Jim was right-handed, so she had Delores sit to the left, where it would be easier to ignore her sourpuss. Bette liked the idea of sitting right next to him: every time he would reach for his drink, she would be sure her hand would be near his.

"Have you ordered, yet?" asked Jim.

Delores responded without looking at him. "Nope, that ditzy waitress hasn't even given us the time of day."

Jim took control. Leaning back in his chair, he shot his long arm straight up into the air. He was 6 foot 3 and lanky, so he seemed even taller. Bette had once referred to him as a "treetop lover" but both Brenda and Delores gave her disapproving looks. They didn't want to think of him in that way. Bette tried to back out of it by saying she was only quoting a song. Delores and Brenda shrugged, not so much because they didn't remember the song, but because they didn't care.

Jim's sudden arm movement and the flash of his bright white shirt sleeve rocketing towards the ceiling caught the eye of the waitress. She smiled at him as she took the order of a heavy-set man who was in a group of ten whose conversations provided most of the noise in the Saloon. She popped up her index finger at Jim, communicating the universal 'Be there in a minute.'

"Well, that seemed to work." Feeling expansive, both physically and emotionally, Jim spread his arms out to his sides, as if to embrace the table of three women. "So, what are you having? Cause I'm buying."

Delores leaned away from one arm, while Bette leaned towards the other, hoping he'd touch her shoulder.

Brenda spoke up, "I feel like havin' one of them frozen drinks, you know, like a margarita or a daiquiri or a piña colada."

"That be fun." Delores actually smiled. Almost.

But Bette threw water on the fun. "They don't have no such thing in this place. You think you in a Caribbean resort. This is a man's bar, this is a gin joint, this is a roadhouse on the side of a road."

Jim was curious why the women suddenly adopted more of an ethnic patois when they spoke to each other in the Saloon. They didn't do that at the supermarket. He decided to play the smart knowledgeable boss but made note to be more casual in his speech. "Let me give you some good news and bad news. Bad news: there ain't no frozen drink machine. And I'm sure our friend Tongue –"

All three women interjected, "Eeewww."

Jim was thrown off by their reaction but continued "— but you can always have a margarita on the rocks. They're quite good. And yes, as a roadhouse, it's meant to be a man's bar. Beer, beer and more beer. But as you can clearly see, tonight there are more women than men."

They all looked around. It was true, but only because of that group of 10 included six women.

Just then, the waitress came over, thinking they were all looking at her, wondering where she'd been. "Hi, y'all. I'm so sorry. We've been real busy."

Delores mumbled, "You call this busy?" but no one heard.

"My name is Marilu, what can I get you?"

What started then became a pattern over the next three hours. Brenda ordered a margarita on the rocks with salt, Delores wanted the same, Bette asked shyly for a rum and Diet Coke, with a lime, and Jim went with a light beer on draft.

The first round broke the ice for the fellow supermarket employees. Brenda was emphatic in her praise of Mr. Jim's recommendation for the margarita. "On the rocks! That's how I drink 'em from now on. On the rocks. Oooo-wee!"

Delores snapped off a zinger, "Like the rocks in your head!" They all laughed. She wasn't being mean – her margarita was already half-gone – she was actually warming up.

Jim wouldn't have noticed one way or the other. Bette was commanding his attention with a little demonstration about how she liked to suck on the wedge of lime that had soaked up all that sweetness from the rum and the soda. She made a big show about biting into the wedge, then licking her lips. Jim might have felt a little uncomfortable with the overt sexuality of Bette's performance, given that she was 20 years his senior, but, with a pint of beer already in him, he started to appreciate how good-looking Bette still was.

It was during the second round that Delores really came alive because the jukebox caught her ear. A couple of older dance tunes came on and that put her in the mood to get up and move. Not that she would ever ask Jim to dance, but she did ask Brenda and Bette. Neither was in the mood – just yet. Brenda was enjoying swaying to the music while still safely in her chair, and Bette started to wonder if she could get Jim to dance with her and hold her close.

There was no designated dance floor in the Saloon, but that never prevented patrons from dancing anywhere and everywhere. On any given night, just the right song on the jukebox could get a few people – sometimes in couples, but mostly solo acts – up on their feet and moving. Always singing along or trying to. And if it was a guy doing the performance, it was guaranteed to involve some air guitar. Folks in Babel weren't necessarily shy about dancing in the Saloon, they just didn't care enough to do it in a community way. So, Tongue never put in a dance floor.

Marilu the waitress was responsible for the music in the jukebox, and it always gave her a little smile whenever someone got up and danced to one of the songs she ordered for the machine.

Jim finally made notice of Delores and, being very insightful about her feelings, handed her a five-dollar bill. "Delores, I love music, too. Why don't you go play some songs? Anything you want. Maybe something to get your friends up and dancing."

Delores broke out a big smile. "I'll go do that. Thank you, Mr. Jim." She stood to go to the jukebox, but first she took a big swig of her third margarita, thinking, 'Somehow that waitress girl, Marilu, she knows exactly when to bring the next round.'

None of the women ever had an empty glass, none of them had a chance to get thirsty. And none of them noticed Jim's little signal to Marilu to order each new round: just eye contact and a whirl of his index finger. He wasn't looking for trouble, he just enjoyed the power of being the man getting the check.

The fourth round finally drove Brenda out of her seat to join Delores in some good-time dancing to an old Motown classic. Thinking she wouldn't be seen, Bette put her hand on Jim's thigh and leaned over to ask him if he was ever going to ask her to get up and dance.

Well aware of the hand on his leg, the rum on her breath, the proximity of Bette's lips to his face, and most importantly the fourth pint (half empty) sitting before him, Jim decided, 'Forty something ain't too old.' But no way was he getting up to dance.

He leaned over to Bette and whispered in her ear, very softly, making sure his lips touched her. "Sorry to disappoint you, but I won't dance. Here. Maybe there's something else we can do."

When he leaned back in his chair, he wouldn't look

over at her, in case the others were watching, or anyone else for that matter. He wanted them to think that anything he might have said to Bette was uninteresting, innocent and sober. He took his time watching Delores and Brenda dance – well, actually they were just swaying, their feet were locked in place to ensure neither would tip over. Then Jim moved his glance over to Bette.

To his shock, she was staring at him. Eyes ablaze, lips gripped tightly over teeth that were clearly clenched. Bette leaned in and spit quietly at him, "What the fuck you mean 'something else we can do'?!"

Jim almost wet his pants. His mouth opened and he stuttered, hoping words would come. Finally, after what felt like a lifetime, he uttered, "I meant like play pool or darts." He wanted to sound as naïve as possible. "I'm really good at both of them."

Bette had had her fun. She smiled broadly and came at him with a big voice, "Why didn't you say so! I love to play pool. Let's do it."

Jim reached for his glass but saw his hand trembling and dropped it down. "In a minute. Let me just run to the men's room." Not waiting for permission, Jim bolted from the table.

When the Motown song ended, Delores and Brenda sat back down and got to work on finishing their drinks. The energy of the music pumped them up further. Shaking her empty glass, Brenda announced yet again, "I love these rocks!"

"Shoot, girl, you love your tequila, that's what you love!" Delores sucked the last of her drink through the straw loudly.

Jim was back and standing above the table. "Have fun dancing?"

"Sure thing. More fun with a margareee-ta." Delores tried to roll the R with a failed Mexican accent. "Maybe one more, but then that's it."

Jim knew one more was already too late for 'one too

many,' but he felt cornered and somewhat obligated. "Okay, one more round, but then I need to head home. It's late, and I have to check in early at the supermarket tomorrow."

Bette looked up at him and saw that there was water dripping from his chin and ears, and the collar of his shirt was wet. He must have gone into the men's room and splashed a gallon of water on his face to sober up. What was he thinking, flirting with an employee nearly twice his age? She smiled to herself, 'musta scared him something shameful.'

Jim caught Marilu's eye and gave her the signal for another round, followed quickly by a pantomimed check mark, the universal 'high sign' for 'time to get going.'

Once he sat done, Brenda, full of tequila and confidence, started in on him. "Why you going home so early? You a young man. It's a Saturday night. It's a holiday weekend. First of all, you shouldn't be out here with us old women anyway. You should be out prowling like a tomcat."

"A tomcat!" That just broke up Delores. She started giggling and cackling and then coughing.

Marilu appeared with another tray of drinks, and Delores grabbed her margarita for a quick sip through the straw. That settled her as she caught her breath. "Tomcat. That's a good one."

Marilu and Jim looked at each other and shared a moment, acknowledging that he had his hands full now. She gave him a wink and slipped him the bill very discreetly. After she left, Bette, who watched that little interaction, gave an audible grunt of displeasure. She mumbled, "Hussy," but no one cared.

Brenda went on, refueling with her fresh drink, "Hush now, let me talk to Mr. Jim. Talk some sense to him." She reached over to take his hand and would have knocked over his new pint if he hadn't swooped it away at the last second. "Listen to me. Don't you want to get married?

65

Don't you want a family? I know you ain't gay. Get your ass out at night and find yourself a woman. Not a woman, like us. But a young girl, you know, good stock, like they say. Shouldn't be out carousing with us. You should be out making flippy floppy."

That just killed Delores. She spit out half her drink. "Bahaha! Flippy floppy!"

Even Bette lost it. She slapped her hand onto the table. Loudly. Three times. "Flippy floppy. Brenda, girl, you crazy."

Jim wanted to climb under the table. He could feel everyone in the Saloon looking over. No matter how loud the jukebox, he knew everyone could hear this new mantra of the three drunk women carrying on with their white boss. He needed to defuse it immediately, no matter what the consequences. Very soberly he said, "Brenda, thank you for your concern. Not that it's anyone's business, but I do have a steady girlfriend. Please excuse me while I go pay our bill." He quickly retreated and went to the bar where he spoke with Marilu and presented her with his credit card.

Back at the table, Delores hissed at Brenda, "Now you did it. You hurt his feelings. And there he was, buying us drinks all night like the best boss we ever had."

Brenda felt badly, but she was a little too drunk to clearly understand why she was feeling badly.

Bette leaned back and announced, "Sisters, this was one fine time we had tonight that we ain't ever gonna have again."

Brenda looked at her drunkenly, "Well we couldn't have it again because it wouldn't be tonight. Tonight can only be tonight, it can't be another night."

Delores smiled. "I don't know what she means, but I'm sure she's right."

Jim was back at the table. "Ladies, it's already after midnight. I called Babel Taxi to send a car to take y'all home. I've had a wonderful time. Thanks for coming out,

I'll see you all tomorrow at three. I know I can count on you to be on time." And with that, Jim gave a slight bow and exited.

The women were so flummoxed that they didn't notice he had gone to the back room and not out the front door.

Unceremoniously, Bette, Brenda and Delores weaved their way through the bar, giving polite 'Good nights' to the waitress, and several of the other patrons. As they passed the bar, Tongue was there wiping the counter. He gave them a big smile and "Thank you for coming by." The trio was polite with their thank yous and good nights but each kept her eyes down.

Outside Delores threw up behind the waiting taxi.

Tongue's Tale 6

Oddest thing. I fell asleep on the beach in Mexico this one time and woke up with a huge sun blister on the tip of my tongue. Mexican doctor said he had no choice but to clip my tongue for fear that an infection might spread and kill me. Wish I remembered what I was dreaming about to make me stick my tongue out.

I GET WILD (11:45 PM)

Just before midnight on the Saturday of Labor Day weekend, the Reillys glided into Tongues Saloon – the only place still open in Babel – feeling very good about their lives and Life in general. They made a quick assessment of the crowd – light for a weekend, but to be expected because of the holiday, with most people being away – then they took up a very familiar position on two bar stools just to the left of the four beer taps.

Tongue, the bartender and proprietor, immediately greeted them. "Well, where you two been? I thought maybe you left town for the weekend?"

"Not us," answered Mark, "we're done with summer vacation. I think Europe for a month was enough, don't you?"

"Hello, Mr. Thomas." Megan – Mrs. Reilly – wedged her heels onto the round metal rung that circled the legs of the stool and in one fluid move, rose up and leaned forward to kiss Tongue on the cheek, balancing herself with one hand flat on the bar while the other smoothed her short skirt in the back. Her husband Mark enjoyed the view of her hand gliding over her perfect posterior. In fact, the scene of his wife kissing the bartender – their old friend – afforded Mark a well-appreciated peek at the alluring trim of Megan's body, not at all hidden by her loose blouse and tight skirt.

"Good to see you, Meg. What can I pour you guys?"

Megan gushed, "We just came from a dinner up in North Babel, at Marr's Bistro, you know it?"

"Oh yeah, heard that's good. 'Out-of-this-world' good. Get it?"

Mark got it right away. "Ouch, man, that was 'out-of-this-world' bad."

"Anyway," Megan continued, her words rushing together, "we were with the Reynolds and the Richters. You know them?"

"Nope." Tongue gave a quick glance to one corner of the bar where Marilu the waitress was processing a tab for a young man who'd been treating three women co-workers to a loud night of fun and drinks.

"Well, after dinner – you know, we had four bottles of wine with dinner – but after dinner, we just sat around and chatted and chatted, and the waiter kept pouring coffee and more coffee and I kept drinking and drinking, and now I've got a caffeine buzz that's going to keep me awake for days."

Mark jumped in, "So we need a night cap to take the edge off. Slow her down. Otherwise she's going to be a zombie."

"I'd say that I could make you a zombie," Tongue joked, "but I have no idea what's in one."

"Nah, I just need a nice after dinner drink," said Megan. "A digestif, as they say."

"Who says that? No one says that," Mark teased.

"Sure they do. An aperitif is for before dinner, and a digestif is for after."

"So, foreplay is an aperitif," Mark suggested, "and a cigarette is for after."

Megan scoffed at him. "A cigarette? That's so cliché. *Cuddling* is the right digestif."

"Well, Tongue, then please pour Megan a glass of cuddle. As for me, I'll have a vodka martini."

Tongue laughed. "One martini coming up. Let me check on our supply of cuddle." Tongue turned away to retrieve a martini glass, not something often used in his bar, but earlier that night, a heavy-set fellow had ordered several Cosmopolitans, yet another new challenge for Tongue.

Megan looked at Mark, all curious. "A martini? That's no digestif."

"Nope. It's what comes right before."

She gave him a poke in the ribs with a whisper, "You mean, it's your sex drink."

"That's right. Because I like it neat. You know, straight up. A stiff drink with maybe a little twist."

Megan giggled and leaned over to her husband, sliding her hand onto his bar stool for balance, her hand between his legs, but not touching him. She said close to his face, "Maybe I'll give you a little twist when we get home."

"Oh, I'm counting on it."

Megan kissed Mark on the mouth, darting her tongue in for a quick tease.

Mark considered grabbing her right then and there and prolonging the kiss, but he knew that it was best to wait for the pay-off back home.

Tongue returned with a short glass of a fiery looking liqueur. "Meg, I thought you might like a glass of amaretto."

"Oh, that's perfect. The liquor of love. *Amore*, as they say."

"Who says *amore*?" Mark quipped. "No one says *amore*."

"I'm pretty sure Italians say it," Tongue responded. He gently placed Mark's martini in front of him, careful not to spill on the trademark coaster that displayed the Saloon's logo: a Rolling Stones-style smiling mouth with the tip of the tongue cut off.

"*L'amour.* That's the right word." Mark leaned towards Megan. "*L'amour* means passion.'"

Megan winked at her husband, but turned to her friend, "Hey, Tongue, how did you know that amaretto would be the right choice?"

Tongue scratched his head, not thinking about the right

answer, but thinking about whether to confess the answer. He saw curiosity in Mark's eyes, so he thought it smart to share what he considered to be valuable information. With a shrug, he admitted, "It's what Marilu drinks when her shift's over and everyone's gone."

"Really." Megan was surprised and thoughtfully assessed this information. She added, innocently, "Kind of lonely to end your night with a love potion, then going home alone."

"Maybe." Tongue moseyed away from Megan and Mark with a poker face they didn't typically see. They watched as Tongue met up with Marilu at the end of the bar who asked him to look for a tea bag.

Megan whispered to Mark. "You think he's got it going on with Marilu?"

"God, I hope so."

"What? Why do you say it like that?"

"I hope someone's got it going on with her. You have to admit, she's some piece of ass."

Megan punched Mark hard on the thigh.

"Ow. What was that for?"

"I'm the only piece of ass you should be hoping about."

"Ah, come on. You can't be jealous. She's just a waitress. She can't hold a candle to you."

Meg stared at Mark, shaking her head in mild disbelief. "What does that even mean?"

Mark stared back at his wife for a few moments. "I really don't know. I never thought about it before. I don't have a clue. I've used that expression my whole life, and I'm just now realizing that I don't know what it could possibly mean." Mark turned and gave his martini some consideration. He took a long sip.

Megan watched him. "Well, I'm sure it must have something to do with beauty being seen as a type of radiance. Whether it's celestial, you know, like the sun. Or holy, like a saint. You know, someone who just radiates goodness, which is a form of beauty, I guess. And trying to hold a candle to that person is like trying to add to your own beauty, or goodness, I guess, to, you know, compete with that person."

Mark wiped his mouth with a cocktail napkin. "Maybe it has to do with worthiness. Like the lesser person isn't even worthy to hold a candle next to the better person to see her better. Or him."

Megan looked at Mark. "Nah, I don't think so. I like mine better."

Mark smiled. "I like yours better, too. In fact, I'd like to hold a candle to you so I can see it better."

Megan laughed and pushed his shoulder away. "Don't start."

"Maybe you'd like me to hold a candle to you and let the wax gently drip …"

"Okay, cut that out. We're here for a night cap. Not for… *amore.*"

"You mean, '*l'amour.*'"

"Nope, I mean what I say and I say what I mean."

"You don't mean that."

"Don't be mean. You know what I mean."

"Sure I do. Say something once, why say it again?"

They smiled at each other. Megan held up her glass of amaretto. "Cheers."

Mark gently tapped her glass with his. "Here's looking at you, looking at me, looking at you. Kid."

Megan smiled as she took a long sip. Putting down her drink, she asked, "Do you think the Reynolds and Richters get our sense of humor at all?"

"Maybe half the time they get about 50% of it, but to tell you the whole truth, I don't much get their humor sometimes. That Pete. His jokes are always half-baked at best."

"And Stan, with his pranks, I mean, really. How childish. I wonder sometimes how Pamela can stand Stan." Megan stopped. "That's funny. Maybe she can't stand Stan."

"Does she even understand Stan?"

Megan laughed. "Maybe when she's under Stan. Ding."

Mark and Megan locked eyes for a moment and put on the poker face they saw Tongue wearing earlier. Mark leaned forward and whispered. "Megan, do you think we might be a little drunk? We're starting to seem pretty stupid."

"Maybe. I'm still feeling the caffeine, but you're right. I'm saying stupid stuff. You're laughing at my stupid stuff."

"I'm not laughing."

"What do you call it then when you smile, open your mouth and make that ha-ha sound?"

"That's called me making you feel good so you'll want to sleep with me."

Megan burst out laughing. "As if that's all it took!" She threw her arms around her husband's neck and practically climbed into his lap. "Honey, you don't have to laugh at me to get laid. You just have to look at me."

The couple kissed long and hard, disregarding their central spot in the Saloon, the thought that anyone there might be looking at them, and even the fact that Tongue had come over to stand opposite them and cleared his throat three times to get their attention. "Excuse me, there, young wild couple. There will be no necromancing in this fine establishment. Please. You'll scare away the tourists. They'll think Babel is Sodom and Gomorrah or something." Naturally Tongue was just teasing his friends, but he also knew that such rare public displays of affections ("PDAs" as Marilu called them) had a tendency to make other people actually feel less romantic.

Mark peeled away and laughed, a little embarrassed. "Sorry there, Mr. Thomas. That wasn't necromancing, which, by the way, is about telling the future. What we were doing was just an experiment."

"Experiment?" Tongue was happy to play along.

"Looked like a taste test to me."

Megan plopped back down on her bar stool and threw her arms up with ceremony. "Ta da! Another safe landing." She went deadpan and turned to Tongue. "It was an experiment in gravity. And I'm happy to report that, once again, I survived. Don't you know that whenever I drink amaretto, I get wild."

Mark teased her, "Is that what it was? I thought it might have been me."

Megan flattened her hand on his chest. "You? You are my gravity. My wild gravity. I fall for you every time."

Mark turned to Tongue. "My friend, I love this woman. It's time for the check and for us to take our experiment homeward."

Tongue spread his arms wide on the bar top, pressed his hands down and leaned over towards them to conspire. "Friends, I'll make you this deal. Leave your drinks as is. Promise me you'll get home safe, and the tab's on me."

Megan cooed, "Oh, T-man, you're the best."

"No, I'm not. Mark is. Take good care of him."

And with that, the friends said good night, and the Reillys left the Saloon as happy with their lives as when they entered.

Tongue's Tale 7

I was dating this girl one time. She was learning to be an acupuncturist. I was crazy for her, so I let her practice on me. Let's just say those needles are not meant to go everywhere. The good news is that she never did get her license.

SLIPPERY PEOPLE (8:00 PM)

When the friends of Paul Wesley showed up at Tongues Saloon, they caught the immediate attention of the only people at the bar. Tongue, the namesake proprietor, was behind the bar cutting an orange. Marilu, a young waitress with a radiant smile and a gymnast's body, was switching channels on the two TVs behind the bar to show the night's big games. There was only one customer, an old timer perched on the bar stool closest to the front door. All three gave the group of ten wary smiles, but the bartender did follow up a cheery, "Welcome, friends."

The waitress walked over. "Hi y'all, make yourselves at home. Sit wherever you'd like. Why don't we push together a few tables?"

It was an odd feeling for the group. Each one of them had been there before, at some point or another. They were never regulars, but they realized tonight over dinner at the Village House that, whenever any one of them had been to the Saloon, it had always been with Paul. He wasn't a regular either. It was just a place he'd go a few times a year but never alone. Sometimes he'd bring his wife Jenny and sometimes they'd bring another couple, like Mike and Melanie, a couple whom Paul befriended through the Babel community theatre, or like their next-door neighbors Frank and Lucy Francis. Or sometimes they'd be joined by other neighbors from along Rhodes Lane, a modest street in Babel Heights that ended in a cul-de-sac. They were all couples: Dennis and Beth Black,

Chuck and Barbara Cannon, and Nancy Frost and Debbie Henderson. (The latter weren't sisters, as the children in the neighborhood had come to learn over time.)

Once, Paul and Jenny and all five of the other couples went bowling, down at the Bowl-a-Rama on Route 5. Afterwards, the dozen friends stopped into the Saloon to buy Dennis and Nancy victory beers for their gender-specific high scores.

At dinner at the Village House, on the Saturday night of Labor Day weekend, it was Frank who pointed out that the only time that all of them had been together at the Saloon was after the bowling adventure. "We should go there tonight. Paul would like that."

Whether or not anyone else thought it was a good idea didn't seem to matter. The group moved as a unit that night, and soon they found themselves in the empty bar, pushing together small square tables with red checkered tablecloths to make one long table, to accommodate ten chairs. Frank took the seat at one head, closest to the bar, and looked up at Marilu with a clear glint in his eye.

"Hi Marilu, how you been?"

Lucy found it curious that her husband would know the name of the Saloon's waitress, but then the young woman said to him, "Well, hello, Mr. Francis, good to see you. Enjoying your summer? Guess school starts up again next week, right?" Lucy realized she was just another poor child who had survived her husband's science class.

Frank answered, "That's right, Marilu. Nothing ever changes at Babel High." He could feel a certain itch on the back of his ears, which he knew from 32 years of marriage meant that Lucy was staring a hole in the back of his head. "Marilu, you remember my wife, Lucy."

"Oh sure. Hi there, Mrs. Francis, so nice to see you again."

Lucy gave her a big mother fox smile, "Don't you look great. You graduate college yet?"

"Last year. Feels so long ago."

Frank smiled, "Bet you enjoyed your summer."

"Not really. Most of my friends have moved away from Babel. If I didn't have this job, I'd be bored out of my mind."

"No thoughts about moving away yourself?" asked Lucy.

"Not really, I kind of like it here. I've got my roots and all. And I do have plans, you know, just everything takes time."

"Like getting a drink in this place?"

Marilu snapped her head around toward the rude comment only to break into a big smile. It was Miss Beth Black, Marilu's old high school English teacher, except she was neither old nor a miss. "Why Miss Black, I didn't even see you there?" Beth was seated behind a rather portly middle-aged man whom Marilu did not know. "How are you?"

Another man across from Beth snapped, "Thirsty."

"Oh Marilu, don't mind him," answered Beth. "That's just my husband Dennis being an ass." Dennis feigned shock at his wife's language.

"That's okay. Let me get you all your orders, then I'll be back for a quick how-do-you-do."

Frank said, "That'd be nice. We'll make it easy for you. Just bring a pitcher of beer. Something light. And a carafe of wine. Something white."

"You rhymed, Frank," noted Lucy.

Dennis said dryly, "You sounded like Dr. Seuss. One fish two fish red fish blue fish."

A tall woman at the far corner of the table piped in, "But you were more like, 'Wine, wine, drink some wine, drink some wine with friends of mine.'"

"That's cute," Marilu said with a smile, wondering what kind of weird night it would be. "I'll go get your drinks."

But the portly man suddenly spoke up, "Excuse me. I'd like to have a Cosmopolitan, please. With lemon vodka. And a lemon peel."

"I'm sorry but we don't carry flavored vodkas. And I'm not sure about the lemon. I know we have an orange. Would you care for an orange peel?"

"I'd love one," the man teased, "just not in my Cosmo. Just have the barkeep make it the regular way, you know, with lime."

"Sure thing. Tongue loves making new drinks." And with that Marilu bounced away leaving the group of ten perplexed about what to talk about. They had arrived in four separate cars, Nancy and Debbie having carpooled with Chuck and Barbara, who had one of those SUVs that looked more like a military weapon than a suburban vehicle. As they drove to the funeral home, then to the cemetery, then to dinner, then to the Saloon, Nancy told stories about various funerals she'd attended over the past 25 years, since her first wake, when her college roommate accidentally electrocuted herself while washing a toaster that somehow was still plugged into an outlet. From the front seat, Barbara ooo'ed and ahh'ed and clucked at all the right moments during Nancy's stories, looking for a change of expression in her husband Chuck, who drove on stoically. Debbie, Nancy's partner of a dozen years, had heard each story more than a dozen times, but still managed the politest of smiles. Occasionally she'd correct a detail about a story, keeping to herself her surprise at Nancy's faulty memory. She chalked it up to the prevalence of wine when recounting her stories.

"So Big Mike, you really want to risk a Cosmo in a place like this?" Debbie looked across the table at her chubby friend, who didn't mind the moniker since it had been established when he hit puberty well-before his classmates, shooting up four inches in one summer. But that was some 35 years earlier before anyone could foresee the rotundity of Big Mike as an adult. He worked as the news, weather and traffic reporter for the local radio station that served Babel and its environs. People he'd meet would often cock their heads when Mike spoke because his distinctive voice sounded familiar, but few of them cared enough to ask if they knew him somehow.

Mike responded dryly to Debbie, "Yes, this is a dive. A roadhouse for the trucker. But still. A Cosmo. It's a shot of vodka, cranberry juice and triple sec, and God willing, a lime. The girl confirmed they have vodka, and it's a bar so they must have triple sec. You can almost smell the cheap margaritas in the air. The risk is, will they have cranberry? My fear is that they'll use ketchup."

That broke up the group into a hearty laugh. They were all on edge because of the funeral, and even the slightest silliness would break the ice and relax them a little. Dennis tried to prolong the laughter, "Or catsup. This bar looks like it's more of a catsup place than a ketchup place."

"Catsup! No one really says 'cat-sup.'" Barbara tried to reason with Dennis while the others laughed along. "Even when the label says 'catsup,' people still say 'ketchup.'"

From the opposite corner of the table, Melanie chimed in, "That's not true. I have cousins who grew up, oh I don't know, a good three hours north of Babel, up in Tottensville, they always said catsup."

"There is no accounting for taste," snickered Dennis.

"Or cousins." Melanie winked at Dennis.

"Or families in general," said Barbara, with more of a sigh than a smile. She was the only stay-at-home mom in the group, so she was particularly sensitive to families.

At the far end of the table, Chuck, who owned his own moving and storage company, stretched out his long arms, "That's why we've got friends."

"Funny, that's something Paul always said, isn't?" Debbie spoke to her hands, folded neatly on the table.

Looking at her partner, Nancy said, "Plenty of times."

"Who could blame him," Lucy cackled. "What with his family."

Beth smiled, "Especially compared to the quality of his friends, right?"

Frank stretched out his arms, mimicking Chuck. "We're here, aren't we?"

"Yes, we are. Drinking," declared Chuck. "Just the way Paul would want it."

"We're not drinking yet," snapped Dennis. He was a salesman for a software company and was accustomed to entertaining, and being entertained, in places fancier than the Saloon.

The group grew silent again. Frank looked around and said dismissively, "Boy, this place is dead."

"How apropos." Mike sounded snarkier than he intended, but his tone was ignored as Dennis weighed in, "He's right. McCormick's Funeral Home was more lively."

"Why is it called a funeral home?" asked Lucy, in the inquisitive voice that warned the employees at First National Bank of Babel where she was an assistant manager that Lucy had found a problem that demanded a clear resolution. "It's not a home. People don't live there. People die there. Why is it called a home?"

Mike corrected her, "Actually, they don't die there, they're dead there."

"I knew a guy who died in a funeral home," said Nancy, almost cheerfully. "It was at a wake. Massive heart attack."

"Do you think it was a broken heart from grief?" Beth was genuine in her question.

"Nah. It was his wife's cousin's husband," Nancy explained. "Just a heart attack. His number was up."

"And that's another thing, what's with this number?" Lucy implored the group.

Frank looked at his wife sideways, "What's the matter, worried yours is too low?"

"I'm just curious where it comes from, and why does it go up? Is it down right now?"

Marilu returned with a tray of glasses. "I brought five beer and five wine. I wasn't sure who was drinking what."

The group was silent while she left and immediately returned carrying a plastic pitcher of foamy-headed beer and a long-necked carafe of white wine. "Here you go. And the Cosmo is coming right up."

Frank took charge of the pitcher and started to pour out glasses for Dennis, Chuck and Barbara, who had each raised their hands in response to Frank's action. Meanwhile, Debbie asked, "Who's drinking wine?" and she did the honors for the four women who spoke up: Melanie, Lucy, Nancy and Beth.

Marilu was back with the Cosmo for Big Mike, which she delivered with special fanfare, since the cocktail was brimming at the top of a martini glass. "And here you go. Careful not to spill. You might want to take a sip first. Hope you like it."

Frank noted that Marilu seemed genuinely nervous. Mike offered a weak smile, not doing a very good job of hiding his apprehension about the quality of the drink, though he was fairly certain it contained neither ketchup nor catsup. He leaned over the drink and took a quick sip to appease the waitress who watched like a mother hen. Mike flashed her a smile of approval and said, "Thank you."

Marilu was pleased and said to the group, "Cheers, everyone. Just call me if you need anything." She nearly skipped back to the bar to report the Cosmo success to the bartender. Chuck watched her go, barely suppressing a leer he hoped his wife wouldn't notice. But Barbara was also watching Marilu, so she did notice when the Saloon door opened and Jed Ellison walked in. Jed owned Harrison's Hardware. Seeing him Barbara turned to her husband and slapped him on the arm, "You need more screws."

Chuck deadpanned, "You read my mind."

"What?"

Chuck spotted Jed and rebounded. "Hardware store. Bag of screws. I get it. But the store's obviously closed now, if he's in here."

"Just don't forget."

Chuck sipped his beer and added a different image to his memory.

At the head of the table, Frank raised his glass and his voice, "Friends. A toast to Paul. He was a good guy. He was a good friend. We're all going to miss him. To Paul."

"To Paul," the group echoed in response. They all sipped their drinks.

Then Debbie spoke up. She and Nancy owned Babel's bookstore, which turned a profit only because they also sold greeting cards, gift wrap, arts and crafts, pottery, and homemade ice cream in the summer and homemade soup in the winter. They kept adding items to ensure that Babel townsfolk would have a reason to drop by. The store was closed today on account of the funeral, and when Debbie spoke up, she felt a certain weight of the day. "I'm not sure if this is appropriate for a toast, but let's just keep Jenny in mind tonight."

"You're so right," said Lucy. "Let's give her a toast for all that she's going through."

"To Jenny," said Melanie, "our friend."

"Jenny," the group echoed in response. They all sipped their drinks again.

Then a silence fell upon them like fatigue, and they quietly let the alcohol swim about their minds for a bit.

Eventually Chuck spoke up, "Boy, this place is dead." His comment just hung in the air, making him feel awkward. Barbara wondered if she should share his shame.

Mike responded to Chuck, but addressed his cocktail, "As if they knew."

Next to him, his wife Melanie shot him a look, "Who knew what?"

He answered simply, "You know."

Debbie jumped in, "I don't know what *they* know, but what *I* know is that it's Saturday night of Labor Day weekend, most everyone goes away."

"Besides, it's early still," added Dennis.

Beth said, mostly to the glass of wine before her, "We never go away."

Dennis retorted dryly, "Well, good thing we didn't have plans for this weekend."

Nancy snapped, "Yeah, that would have been inconvenient."

Dennis felt horrible. "I didn't mean it like that."

"We were going to go away." Everyone looked at Barbara as she continued. "Thursday night our bags were packed. We were going to visit Chuck's brother down at the lake. He's got a house."

"What lake?" asked Lucy.

Chuck chimed in, "Lake Legba. My brother's got a boat. Would have been a little fishing, a little water skiing. Lots of beer."

"Nice." Dennis then asked, "What's your brother do?"

Chuck stared at him without answering. He seemed to be searching for the right word.

Barbara reached over and placed her hand on Chuck's. She answered for him, addressing the group. "Chuck's brother, James, owns a funeral home."

"He's an undertaker?" asked Dennis.

"Yeah," Chuck sipped his beer.

Barbara clarified, "James runs a funeral home in East Zimbra. He took over the business from Chuck's grandfather."

Chuck smiled wryly, "I come from a long line of undertakers."

Frank tried to lighten the mood, "I hear people are dying to get into the business."

Mike said, "Good one," not meaning it in the least.

The silence returned to the group as they all wondered about being an undertaker, or the convenience of having one in the family – or was it an embarrassment? They wondered about the awkwardness of talking about the trappings of death on the day of Paul's burial, and they wondered about the coincidence of life and death being woven together in the everyday of people's thoughts and words.

"I grew up saying 'funeral parlor' not 'funeral home.'" It was Lucy trying to shift the awkwardness by prolonging it.

"Parlor? You mean like 'ice cream parlor'?" asked Dennis. "Never heard of it. Funeral home, that's what I know."

Debbie said, "I remember 'funeral parlor,' but that's old school. No one has parlors anymore."

"Just parlor games," added Beth.

Nancy teased, "Maybe if we click our heels three times and say, 'There's no place like a funeral home, there's no place like a funeral home,' instead of dying, we just wake up in Kansas."

Mike leaned past Beth to poke at Nancy, "Same difference." He leaned back and sipped his Cosmo, smug with the thought of his superior wit.

Just then the front door to Tongues Saloon opened, and the ten friends all turned to watch as a woman in her forties entered, trailed closely by a young man, clearly her son. After a second or two, a pair of men followed them in. But the men took stools at the bar, and the mother and son headed for a table in the corner of the main room, furthest from the group. No one in the group thought the pursuit of privacy to be odd, but they all were surprised by the unexpected site of a mother and son in a drinking establishment.

"That's Peggy," said Frank. "You know, Gasoline Peggy."

"Don't tell me that's Colin," said Lucy in an exaggerated whisper.

Debbie commented, "Damn, he's the spitting image of his father."

"Is he? I never knew him," said Mike, peering over at

the young man.

"Why do people say that?" asked Lucy.

"He's dead now, what? Twenty years?" Nancy wondered aloud.

Frank leaned in, "Got to be longer. She was pregnant with Colin when Liam was killed."

Lucy shook her head, "But why do people use that expression? It's weird. And disgusting."

Frank looked at his wife, "What are you talking about?"

"Debbie said Colin was the spitting image of his father. Why is it called the 'spitting image'?" Lucy looked at Mike, expecting him to know.

Mike smirked, "I don't have a clue."

"Once again admitting you're clueless," Melanie teased. She smiled to herself: as a real estate agent she had to be nice to people all day long, so her relief valve was to tease her husband. Relentlessly.

From across the table, Dennis admired the marital sting. "Nice one, Mel. You go girl."

Beth preferred to keep her husband out of other couples' conversations. "Yeah, I don't know why it's called spitting image, and, as the man said, frankly, I don't give a darn."

Nancy looked at her, "Hunh? Don't give a darn about what?"

"Spitting images," Beth stated.

"Who's splitting?" asked Chuck. As the conversation had meandered along the table, some context was lost among the friends.

Debbie tried to help him out. "No one's splitting. And no one's spitting, either."

Feeling lost, Chuck offered, "Well, that's good."

Feeling left out, Chuck's wife Barbara jumped into the conversation. "Who are the two new guys at the bar?"

"Don't you know Gus the electrician?" Melanie said with surprise.

"That's Gus?!" Debbie said in her own surprise. "He

looks like he lost a lot of weight."

Melanie assessed Gus seated at the bar. "Maybe."

Lucy blurted out, "I can't get over how grown up he looks."

"Gus? He's nearly fifty!" exclaimed Debbie.

"No. Colin."

Melanie stared at Lucy, "Who was talking about Colin?"

"I'm just saying," Lucy said sheepishly.

"Okay, try to stay with us, Lucy." Frank spoke condescendingly to his wife of three decades. "We were talking about Gus."

Lucy confirmed, "The electrician."

"The only Gus in here," said Frank.

Mike sat a little taller and asked Frank, "Do you know the guy he's talking to?"

Frank looked over at the bar, "No, I don't think so."

Mike smiled, "Maybe his name is Gus too, so then Gus the electrician wouldn't be the only Gus in here." Mike beamed.

Frank smiled at him. "Do you know if anyone in here is named Richard?"

Mike looked around, "I don't think so."

"Then that makes you the only Dick in here."

The group burst out laughing, even Big Mike himself. They all knew each other well enough to know exactly which buttons to push, and which lines couldn't be crossed. The friends would all happily skate along those lines, cheerful in their constant teasing, joyful in each other's embarrassment, knowing the comeback will be just as amusing.

Mike toasted Frank, "Well done."

Frank, still smiling, said, "I can't take the credit for that one. Learned it from Paul. Saw him use it years back. Great zinger."

"He was the best at it," admitted Melanie.

Frank pointed out, "Couldn't take them as well, though."

"That's true," agreed Lucy. "He was a softy."

Debbie jumped in. "I think there was a whole lot going on to explain all that he was."

"True of anyone," said Mike.

Lucy asked, "What do you think it's like, growing up without a dad and your mom having your dad's job?"

Everyone looked at Lucy, who was staring across the room.

"You back on young Colin again?" asked Frank.

"Just wondering," answered Lucy.

Debbie commented, "I remember thinking at the time, his father's death was going to destroy this town."

Melanie said, "We were all numb for quite a while after he was killed."

Barbara leaned in. "Obviously Chuck and I weren't around back then. Tell us the story."

"When did you move to Babel?" asked Big Mike.

Barbara told him, "Same year as Paul and Jenny."

Melanie noted, "That was about ten years ago."

"That's right," Chuck said. "It was the summer that Joey Botts cut down the climbing tree and Psycho died."

Dennis slapped the table, "You're right. We had those sandy clams that summer."

Beth looked at her husband in amazement. "Wait a minute. You remember something you ate ten years ago? Something as mundane as clams."

Dennis defended himself, "It all ties together."

"I'm sure it does," Beth smirked. "Please, enlighten us."

Big Mike barked, "Don't feel obligated."

Melanie snapped at him, "Mike, be quiet and let him tell the story."

Dennis began, "Ten years ago, for Beth's thirty-third birthday, we had a barbecue in our backyard."

Beth interrupted, "You could have said 'birthday.' The number is irrelevant."

Dennis ignored his wife with a smile. "It was a

Saturday afternoon. Beautiful July day. When we hear this buzzing sound, you know, like a weed whacker. But we knew it was something different. I was kind of ticked that someone would be doing landscaping when we were having a party. But of course, all the neighbors were at the party. Except for Joey Botts. But we never invited him to anything."

"Who was Joey Botts?" asked Melanie.

"Joseph Botticini." Frank enjoyed emphasizing each syllable.

Lucy blurted out, "Joey Botts. It's fun to say."

"Got it," said Big Mike impatiently. "But who was he?"

Dennis spoke to Mike and Melanie across the table. "He lived in the corner house before Chuck and Barbara moved in."

Barbara corrected him, "Actually we bought it from the Lebanese family who bought it from Botticini."

"Oh right, the Lesbos!" Nancy elbowed Beth.

She replied, "I forget, why did they move?"

It was Debbie who answered. "Family thing. They weren't in that house for more than six months. A shame. They seemed like nice people."

Nancy nearly shouted, "The wife made amazing baba ghanouj. To die for!"

Chuck asked, "What's baba ghanouj?"

Barbara looked at her husband, "Don't you ever get out?"

Chuck smiled, "Only when you walk me."

"Excuse me." Big Mike tried to restore order to the conversation that pinballed along the table. "Joey Botts? I believe once upon a time he cut down a tree. Can we finish one story tonight?"

Beth joked, "I cannot tell a lie. Joey Botts cut down the climbing tree."

Dennis nodded appreciation to Mike. "So, I leave the birthday party to see what's the noise and swear to God, there's Joey with a freakin' chainsaw, cutting down the climbing tree."

Seeing blank stares on several faces across the table from her, Nancy explained: "The climbing tree was right in the middle of Joey's front yard. It was this beautiful evergreen that had long strong branches that started off low on the trunk. So all the neighborhood kids would climb it. But Joey Botts being either on the lam or in witness protection or…"

"Or just a creep," added Beth.

Nancy continued, "He didn't want kids on his property. So instead of talking to his neighbors, he cut down the tree."

Mike asked Dennis, "And?"

"And what?"

"You were going to tie this into the Wesleys moving onto the block."

Melanie reminded them, "And Psycho getting killed."

"Of course." Dennis tapped his temple, the universal mea culpa for forgetting. He continued, "A few weeks later, Paul and Jenny and their kids, they only had two at the time, move in, and because the tree is still lying in the street in front of Joey's house…"

Beth quickly jumped in, "Joey wouldn't pay to have the tree removed, so he cut it up with his chain saw and left it at the curb. It was a mess all summer."

Dennis went on, "Anyway. Psycho, that was a stray cat that sort of guarded the block…"

Debbie announced, "He was our unofficial mascot and we all unofficially fed him."

Lucy admitted, "We used to leave a saucer of milk at the back door for him."

"You did. I didn't." Frank grimaced. "I don't like cats."

Mike winked at Frank, "What you got against cats?"

"Long story."

Melanie whispered to Frank, "Can't be longer than this one."

"Anywho," Dennis tried to get everyone's attention again. "Psycho was stalking a mouse or something in the wood pile that was once Joey's tree, when he suddenly dashed into the street just as the moving truck for Paul and Jenny was backing up. Killed him dead."

"Psycho or Joey?" asked Chuck, not half-joking.

Barbara snapped at her husband, "Psycho, you idiot."

Chuck shrugged and held out his palms to Barbara, "I was kidding."

"I wasn't," she replied.

"Why was the cat called Psycho?" asked Melanie.

Debbie noted, "Tamest cat in the world, so Psycho was just perfect."

Frank said, with a big smile, "I had suggested Archimedes, but that was already taken."

Mike looked at him, "I don't get it."

Lucy leaned back in her chair, "Frank's real name is Archimedes."

Mike looked at Lucy, then at Frank, then back to Lucy. "You're shitting me."

Lucy laughed, "Trust me, I wouldn't make it up."

Melanie put her hand on Frank's forearm. "I always thought you were Francis Francis."

"Really?" Frank's expression indicated disappointment in the suggestion, and in Melanie.

Big Mike offered, "Or Hot Dog Francis."

Lucy laughed again, "Not likely."

As her laugh trailed off, the group grew silent again, and Chuck took the opportunity to pour out the remainder of the pitcher of beer into Dennis' glass and his own, ignoring his wife's, which was still a quarter full. He discreetly motioned to Frank to order another pitcher, but Beth intercepted his signal.

Looking for the waitress, Beth turned to the bar just as the old man slowly rose from his stool, slapped his hand on the bar, and headed for the door. Leaning towards Lucy, she whispered, "Who is that?"

Lucy checked him out but said, "I don't know him."

Frank added, "I don't know his name, but I've seen him around for years."

"And you never asked anyone his name?" Lucy seemed annoyed.

"No. I never really cared." Without looking at his wife, Frank added sarcastically, "Do you want me to invite him over?"

"No, thanks. I'm sure he has better things to do than meet you." Lucy gave it right back to Frank. "Why don't you invite Marilu over? I bet you'd like that."

"I should. I believe there's a request for more beer at the other end of the table."

Frank polled the group on who needed what for the next round and waved over Marilu.

She returned with her usual smile, this time standing between Frank and his wife, sensing that she was leery of her knowing Mr. Francis. Marilu was also able to see Miss Black better this time, without the round man getting in the way.

As Frank told Marilu the table's orders, Melanie noticed three new arrivals to the Saloon. She elbowed her husband, and Big Mike took his eyes off of Marilu to watch three middle-aged black women quietly cross the room towards a table right in the center of the Saloon, but near the bar. He whispered to Melanie, "That's the crew from the supermarket."

She responded, "I wonder who's minding the store."

Mike noted, "Looks like they're expecting to be the center of attention tonight."

Hearing his comment, Frank said, "They usually are."

"Why do you say that?" asked Lucy.

"Remember that time at the Bowl-a-Rama?" Frank said.

Lucy let out a long low exclamation. "Oooohhhhhh right, that was them."

Melanie laughed. "I forgot about that. That was years ago."

Mike snorted, "Was that before or after Psycho got crushed?"

Melanie looked at Mike, disappointed again. "Really? Hasn't today been enough about death?"

"Sorry." Mike swirled his empty glass, wishing to be somewhere else, even if it was McCormick's Funeral Home.

Marilu delivered a fresh pitcher of beer, a carafe of wine and a second Cosmo for Mike. But despite the natural cheerfulness she brought with her, once she walked away, the group again fell into another wave of silence. They each were aware of the awkwardness, but no one wanted to be the one to risk trying to break the ice and failing.

Beth thought about saying, 'What would Paul say to break the silence?' She thought this could be a fun parlor game, but that made her think about Lucy's 'funeral parlor,' so she changed her mind.

Lucy wanted to ask about Jenny and the kids, but she figured no one knew the answers yet anyway.

Dennis wanted to talk more about Paul's death, but he knew that no way was that a topic for the Saloon on that night.

Chuck was itching to play pool and was wondering how long was proper to wait before suggesting it to Dennis. He made eye-contact with his wife Barbara but couldn't get a sense of her mood or her thinking.

Barbara looked into Chuck's eyes and wished he'd go play pool with the guys. She really wanted to talk to the girls about Paul, and just share her thoughts on him being a good husband and father. She was sure her own husband was tired of that talk.

The group's silence wasn't helped by the lack of noise in the Saloon. No one had ventured to the jukebox yet, and the game on the televisions behind the bar added only a low dull hum behind the soft conversations around the Saloon: the two men at the bar, the mother and son in the corner, and the three newcomers in the middle. Marilu and the bartender would chat at the corner of the bar whenever they could, but still, all the quiet talking in the big room created only a murmur.

It wasn't long before the Saloon's front door opened and a man entered, making a beeline straight for the three women.

Turning to watch him, Frank commented, "Ain't that somethin'. That's Jim Helper. He's the boss at the supermarket."

Melanie asked emphatically, "Who *is* minding the store?"

"Must be closed, since they're all here," said Mike.

Frank said, "It is a holiday weekend. I'm sure they close early."

"How come it doesn't feel like a holiday weekend?" asked Dennis to no one.

But his wife snapped back at him, "Maybe because we buried Paul this morning."

Dennis shot Beth a hurt look. He didn't mean to be insensitive. He thought to himself, 'I just forgot.'

Frank sensed trouble brewing so he took a risk for levity's sake. He lowered his voice and spoke slowly, drawing out his words with a slight tremble, "I buried Paul."

Everyone turned and looked at him. The moment seemed eternal. Frank worried to himself, 'Won't anyone get it?'

Finally, it was Debbie who said, "I never believed it was 'Cranberry sauce.'"

Nancy repeated it for her, mimicking Frank's slow tone, "Cran-ber-ry sauce."

"What are you guys talking about?" demanded Lucy.

Mike looked at her and, trying hard not to sound condescending, said, "Even I know this one. Back in the days of Beatlemania, there was a rumor that Paul McCartney was killed in a motorcycle crash and was quietly replaced by a double."

"Who just happened to be British, could sing, and play bass. Left handed," added Frank.

"Anyway, conspiracy theorists began finding clues in song lyrics and album cover art that 'proved' Paul had died," Mike explained.

Frank continued the thread, "So. At the end of 'Strawberry Fields Forever' – you know the song – a man's voice, probably John's, is heard saying 'I buried Paul.'"

"Or, cran-ber-ry sauce," Nancy intoned.

Lucy struggled with this new information. "If it was Strawberry Fields, why didn't he say, 'strawberry sauce.'"

Frank retorted, "Because he said, 'I buried Paul.'"

"But he didn't bury Paul, I mean, he didn't really die, so why say 'I buried Paul' at all." Lucy went on. "Seems like he would be saying something else like, 'I'm very tall."

Frank looked long at his wife, then announced, "You're out of your mind."

"I'm just saying."

Frank dismissed her. "Well, listen to the song. With headphones. Then decide what he's saying."

Mike mocked Lucy, "I'm – very – tall."

Feeling bad for Lucy, Melanie said, somewhat timidly, "Well John was the tallest Beatle."

Before anyone could challenge her, Chuck blurted out, "I -- buried -- Carl."

The group looked at Chuck in shared confusion. In doing so they missed a young couple – who had just entered the Saloon – walk to the far end of the room and sit at a table for two.

"What did you say?" asked Barbara.

Chuck felt self-conscious, so he whispered to his wife, making everyone else look away out of embarrassment.

"That's Carl Carbone. The guy who just walked in." She looked over and saw the young muscular man sitting with a pretty twenty-something she recognized from the shoe store in town.

Chuck explained, "He works in the building next to me. I see him sometimes at lunch. Sometimes at the gym."

"Are you going to say hello?"

"Nah. He's clearly on a date."

Barbara agreed, "Yeah, that's the girl who manages the shoe store."

Chuck said, "Figures you'd know that."

Barbara chose to ignore her husband and instead watched the waitress scamper between tables to get to the jukebox. Marilu put in her money and banged on the keys so quickly, Barbara realized she must be picking favorites that she knew by heart. Then Marilu slid over to her table of new customers, and Barbara turned her attention back to what Lucy was asking the group.

"Isn't Strawberry Fields the name of the garden in Central Park in New York City where John Lennon is buried?"

Frank nearly dropped his glass of beer. "John Lennon is not buried in Central Park. You can't bury people in public parks."

Big Mike quipped, "What about Grant's Tomb?"

Frank spat back at him, "What about it? It's not in a park."

"Why does it matter?" asked Lucy. "Who's buried in Grant's Tomb?"

Frank started at his wife, "You're kidding me, right?"

Mike leaned in towards Lucy, "I'll give you a hint." Then in a slow drawn-out voice with a slight tremble, Mike uttered, "I – buried – Ulysses."

That broke up the table in laughter again. Except for Lucy, who was feeling baffled.

Nancy jumped back in, "But seriously, I really do think it's 'I buried Paul.' And I do think Paul died somehow."

Beth put her hand on Nancy's arm. "So, you think that the Paul McCartney who's been enjoying life as a former-Beatle, all these years, is not the original Paul McCartney."

Nancy tried to defend herself. "I'm just saying."

"You're just saying what?" Debbie was genuinely annoyed at her partner, but she turned and addressed everyone else. "Why do people say, 'I'm just saying,' when we can all hear them, and we recognize the motion of their mouth and the sound that comes out is called 'saying'?" Debbie flapped her hand in front of her mouth, imitating a duck's beak. "Why say, 'I'm just saying,' when what you're really saying is, 'I've got nothing worth saying.'"

The harshness of her words stunned the group.

After a moment, Nancy mumbled, "Never mind." Then she started to cry.

After another moment, Debbie asked, trying to suppress her annoyance, "Why are you crying?"

Dabbing her eyes with a tissue from her bag, Nancy said clearly, for all to hear, "I miss Paul."

"Now? All of a sudden it hits you?" asked Debbie.

Nancy stared at her. "He would have backed me up."

Again, the awkward silence gripped the ten friends at the table as they each mulled over Nancy's invocation of their dead friend, until Big Mike spoke up, "I don't think so, Nancy. Paul was more of a Stones fan." The joke received smirks but no laughs.

Then Lucy nearly lunged forward with an idea. "Maybe we should create a garden memorial for Paul. You know, like Strawberry Fields Forever."

Frank asked, "Do you think he'd like that?"

Melanie countered, "Doesn't really matter, does it? The question is, would Jenny like it?"

Big Mike muttered, mostly to himself, "All the lonely people, where do they all come from?"

For the next twenty minutes the group debated in earnest the idea of creating a memorial garden in Babel for Paul Wesley. They worried about Jenny's approval, whether it would be a wonderful gesture or a painful reminder for the Wesley children. They fought over where the garden should be placed and how to secure the approval from the town. They speculated about the cost to build it and the cost to maintain it. Ultimately they agreed that it was a heartfelt and loving idea that they'd propose to Jenny in a week's time, after they did some research on how to make it a reality.

But it was Frank who captured the problem the group faced. "What we need is the right person with the vision to create this garden, figure out how to make it happen, and to ensure that it stays beautiful for years to come. And unfortunately, we buried that person today."

There was general agreement around the table with many silent nods and several anxious reaches for glasses to sip from. But by this point all the glasses, as well as the beer pitcher and the wine carafe, were empty. The waitress Marilu had been keeping her distance because of the intensity of the conversation at the table.

Frank held up the empty beer pitcher which caught the attention of the bartender, Tongue, who signaled to Marilu, who was just saying 'Good night, now' to Gasoline Peggy and her son Colin. Frank thought back to when Colin was in his class maybe five or six years back. Frank remembered him as being reclusive, but a good kid. All the teachers had felt bad for Colin – growing up without a father. But everyone thought his mother did a great job of raising the boy and making a success of the gas station as well. 'So, the kid was an introvert,' thought Frank. 'Most high school boys are anyway. No harm in keeping to yourself.' Frank nodded to his empty glass, 'Looks like he turned out alright.'

As Frank watched the pair exit the Saloon, he saw yet another newcomer arrive. A man in his mid-forties. Unshaven but not unkempt. Curious but unremarkable. Out of habit – schoolteachers always monitoring kids' comings and goings against the clock – Frank checked his watch. Just a little after 10. "I guess people drop in at all hours," Frank said to no one.

But Lucy was listening, and the newcomer had caught her eye, too. "Who's that?"

"No one I know."

"What's with the bag?" With a nod of her head, Lucy pointed out the small duffel bag the man carried low in his right hand, as if something long and heavy were inside.

Melanie offered, "Looks like a trucker." She picked up on Lucy's nosiness, but dismissed it, turning her attention to Marilu who arrived with a fresh pitcher and carafe.

"How 'bout something from our 'Bar Eats' menu?" Marilu asked the table. "Y'all hungry?"

Lucy responded, "Oh please, I'm still stuffed from dinner."

Frank suggested, "Could you bring us a couple of baskets of chips or pretzels or popcorn? Something just to snack on."

Marilu said, "Oh sure. We've got all three." Then she put a friendly hand on Big Mike's shoulder, which made his wife smile. "And you, sir. Would you care for another Cos-mo-politan?" In fun, she dragged out the word.

Mike mimicked her in response, "No-mo-politan."

Melanie poked him with her elbow, so Mike said, "Thank you" to Marilu, then added, "But I will have a club soda and lime. When all's said and done, I'm the one driving home."

Marilu smiled and left to fetch Mike's beverage.

"When all is said and done," Beth intoned. "That was one of Paul's favorites."

"You're right," agreed Melanie. "'There's a train leaving nightly called When All's Said And Done.'"

Debbie smiled, "'Keep Me In Your Heart.'"

Frank noted, "Warren Zevon. Before he passed."

"Obviously," said Mike.

"Well, naturally." Frank appreciated the quip.

Debbie wanted to keep it serious for a moment. "Anyway. It was Paul's favorite."

But the moment was lost when Dennis joked, "Was it? I thought he liked 'Free Bird.'"

Nancy spoke up, "Well you didn't hear no 'Free Bird' at

the funeral today, did you?"

"That would have been a nice touch," said Chuck.

Dennis raised his glass and offered a toast, "Free Bird."

Beth responded to her husband by raising her glass and saying, "Whatever."

All the other women at the table raised their glasses and toasted, "Whatever."

Dennis smirked, "Women," and took a long slug of his beer. "On that note, who wants to play some pool?"

Chuck nearly jumped to his feet. "Definitely."

Beth looked at Dennis. "Really?"

But Barbara spoke up, as if excusing both husbands, "It's fine, go ahead."

Chuck called to the other end of the table, "Hey Frank, you in?"

Acting like it was a favor, Frank answered, "Sure, I'm good for a game or two."

Dennis looked at Big Mike. "Mike? How about you?"

Mike laughed. "Nah, I don't think so. Billiards is not my sport. Too strenuous. I better stay here and safeguard the womenfolk." Melanie rolled her eyes.

Just then Marilu delivered Mike's club soda and lime with a – "Here you go, champ." She winked at Melanie as she placed four baskets of snacks on the table, then she quickly returned to the bar.

Dennis whined, "Mike, come on, we need a fourth."

"I'm only on my third," cracked Mike.

Chuck tapped Dennis' shoulder. "Never mind. I'll go ask the hardware store guy if he wants to play."

As Frank and Dennis retreated to the back room of Tongues, with freshly poured beers and a basket of pretzels, Chuck approached the bar. There were only two customers, each seated at opposite ends. Chuck didn't recognize the man at the far end. He thought he looked like a trucker. Unshaven, eyes hidden under his camouflage baseball cap. He seemed to be staring intently into his drink, probably whiskey. Then he took a stub of a pencil out of his shirt pocket and scribbled in a little notebook. Chuck thought this was curious, but he didn't care enough to give it another thought. The guy was just a typical Saloon denizen, and Chuck was eager to play pool.

He approached the 'hardware store guy.' "Hey. It's Jed, right?"

"Yep."

"I know you from the hardware store."

"Sure. You were in last week for the ladder."

"That's right. I'm Chuck." They shook hands.

Jed asked, "How's the ladder working out?"

"I'll let you know once I use it." They laughed.

"Impulse purchase?"

"Not really. I have to put up a new ceiling light fixture." Chuck smirked, "I just haven't gotten to it yet." Then he added, very seriously, "But I do need a bag of screws."

Jed stared hard at Chuck, trying to quickly process whether that was a joke, a request or just a non-sequitur. Safely, Jed offered, "I don't seem to have any on me right now."

Chuck laughed. "No, no. I meant I'll have to come back in. For screws. When you walked in tonight, my wife reminded me that I needed screws."

"Everyone always does." Smiling, Jed took a quick sip of his pint of beer.

"Anyway, I'm playing pool with two of my friends and we need a fourth. Would you be interested?"

"That sounds like an excellent idea." Without a moment's hesitation, Jed scooped up his beer and the pile of cash from his spot at the bar. "Hey Tongue. I'll be shooting pool. But I'll be back."

Tongue, who had been staring intently at the game on one of the TV sets, turned and fired off a thumbs up at Jed, "Good luck. And no gambling, boys. Leads to violence." He smiled and turned his attention back to the game.

Jed followed Chuck to the back room. As he passed the table where Mike and the women sat, Jed made eye contact with Lucy and then Barbara, knowing that they – or their husbands – were customers. Each received his standard polite smile, made a little bit wider with the few beers he'd already had.

With the men vacating three of the seats at the table, the women shuffled the arrangement. Barbara slid over to her husband's chair, putting her next to Debbie and across from Beth. Nancy moved into Frank's seat at the head of the table, saying, "No offense, Beth, I just wanted to be able to hear everyone better. The jukebox can be kind of loud."

For the first time the group paid attention to the music from the jukebox, realizing that it must have been playing for a while without anyone commenting on it. Debbie was surprised and wondered whether her friends had been too wrapped up in their conversations or themselves. "I can't believe we didn't notice the music. What songs have been playing? I couldn't even tell you whether it's been country or rock or whatever."

Mike answered her, "I'll tell you this, it hasn't been jazz."

"Yeah, I don't think you're getting many jazz fans in a saloon like, well, the Saloon."

Mike feigned injury, "I'm here."

"Not by choice," commented Melanie.

Lucy chimed in, "Don't say that. We all chose to come here. For Paul."

"Paul would have liked the music," said Nancy.

Beth pointed out, "Paul would have been at the jukebox all night."

Mike and the six women looked over at the jukebox, each imagining their friend standing there making selections.

As if on cue, one of the three Suprette women who were drinking with their boss weaved her way between tables and chairs towards the jukebox. Debbie figured that, based on the laughter that had been coming from that table, they were having a good time. Nancy figured that, based on the woman's apparent challenge with pushing buttons on the jukebox and staying perfectly upright, she was well on her way to getting drunk.

Lucy said, "Mike, I don't think we'll be hearing jazz any time soon."

The next selection of music began to play, somehow seeming a little louder. The song was familiar to everyone in the group, but not a song any of them felt like hearing.

"This oughta be good," said Melanie with a hint of snarkiness as she watched the jukebox-woman start to dance. 'Well, she's not really dancing,' Melanie thought, 'since her feet are cemented to the floor.' Melanie said to her friends, "It's like she's pretending to surf."

Nancy and Debbie smiled, quite familiar with non-dancing dancing.

Mike turned away and focused on his club soda. In a resigned tone, he announced. "Motown. The Motor City. More hit songs than hit cars."

Beth leaned towards him, "Not if you consider how many cars get hit." She smiled sheepishly at Mike.

He rolled his eyes in response. "Really, Beth, really. I expect better from you."

She patted his shoulder, mockingly, "That's okay, I expect nothing more from you."

That made him laugh.

Debbie caught the exchange and wondered whether any bitterness existed under the constant sniping and teasing her group of friends unleashed on each other. She wondered if she should be worried. She wondered if she should say something. Then she stopped and said to herself, 'I wonder what Paul would do.' Her empty glass stared back at her and suggested an answer.

"Remember the time..." Debbie began one of those quick little anecdotes that everyone remembers quite clearly, but despite that fact, the teller revels in the retelling of the tale, taking her audience along for the ride despite their knowing exactly where they're going. The enjoyment of that ride – the retelling, sometimes with exaggerated facts, but always with exaggerated gestures and dramatic words and sounds and pauses – that ride was a near magical experience for the audience.

For the next half hour, the group of six women, along with Big Mike, shared their memories of their departed friend Paul, with each story snowballing the superlatives of the 'best,' 'funniest,' 'craziest,' and 'my all-time favorite.' The stories rejoiced in the comic things that Paul had said and mis-said, the amazing things he had done and things he had done amazingly poorly, loving things he had done for his wife Jenny and the stories she told lovingly behind his back.

The stories didn't make the group miss Paul any less, as they each felt a deeper appreciation for him. During the thirty minutes, each woman – Debbie, Nancy, Beth, Melanie, Lucy and Barbara – stole a furtive glance around the table, noting a warmth among the friends that always existed but was never felt so keenly before.

Only Mike kept his eyes lowered, staring into his now empty glass, occasionally swirling it, as if some invisible potion remained inside. Across from him, his wife Melanie knew that, despite the shared laughter, Mike was hurting badly. He may have been closest to Paul, and this was the first close death he'd experienced. She worried about Mike. She knew if Paul were there, he'd be able to talk to Mike in a way she couldn't.

Dennis was suddenly at the table, "What are you guys all yucking about? We can hear you laughing in the back room."

Debbie, wiping tears of laughter from her cheeks, started, "Remember the time..."

But the group cut her off, begging her not to start again. Nancy squealed, "My ribs are killing me from laughing. I really think I split my sides."

That set off another round of laughs.

Dennis quickly refilled his glass with beer and poured a refill for Chuck. "Well, you guys have fun. We'll be back." He looked at Beth, "Can you get more snacks?"

She shot back, "How 'bout an order of snacks with a side of manners?"

Dennis smiled widely, "You know, you ought not kid about food with a hungry man who's busy saving the family's honor by kicking some butt in a highly competitive game of pool."

Beth smiled back, looking deeper into his eyes, calculating just how much beer her husband had already consumed and what that might mean for the eventual car ride home and the inevitable wrestling match in bed. "You're right, Fast Eddy, I ought not." She puckered an air kiss at him and politely turned her attention back to the conversation at the other end of the table.

Dennis carried his two beer glasses to the back room, thinking there might be a little reward waiting for him at home because of his charming ways.

It wasn't long before Jed and Frank emerged from the back room. Frank addressed the table, "Well, I've had enough of pool for another decade. Seems I've lost a certain finesse."

Lucy clucked to the table of women, "You're telling me."

Jed clapped Frank on the shoulder, "Ah, you did just fine, Mr. Francis. I'm the one who's a little rusty. Not a good thing in my line of work." He looked at the faces staring at him from the table. Realizing no one caught his little pun, Jed thought it was time to retreat. "Well, I ought to get going."

Beth furrowed her brow, "What's with the 'oughts' tonight?" But no one heard.

Jed continued, feeling he had a stage. "We're open tomorrow. Like every Sunday. You know, the hardware

store. Don't forget your screws. And nails and whatnot."
Embarrassed now, he ended, "Well, good night to you all,"
and headed back to the bar.

The group remained silent, watching as Jed declined the
bartender's offer of another drink, deciding instead to
settle his tab.

Frank announced, "Nice guy. Not much of a pool
player. But nice guy."

Beth said, "Well, he ought to be." But no one heard.

No sooner had Jed walked out, then the young couple
– the woman from the shoe store and the fellow Chuck
knew – left the Saloon as well, which everyone at the table
made note of.

Mike commented, "Hunh. Must have been a first
date."

Lucy opined, "Kind of early to be ending a first date.
Unless it's not going well."

Debbie said, in a conspiratorial tone, "Or maybe it's
going so well, it's time to go to bed."

"Did it go well?" Nancy asked her partner.

"I think yes."

Beth asked, "How can you tell?

"Body language," Debbie answered. "He held the door
for her."

Barbara spoke up, "I know her. She's works at the
shoe store. She's a sweetheart."

"You're right, her name's Donna," added Melanie. "I
think."

Mike asked, "Think she wasn't working tonight because
of the holiday or because she got fired?"

Lucy interrupted, "Who was the muscle man with her?"

Melanie stared at her husband, "What shoe store stays
open late on a Saturday night? She didn't get fired." She
muttered under her breath, "Really."

Mike tried to save face with comedy, "Maybe he's
kidnapping her?"

Nancy tried to diffuse Melanie's annoyance and said to

Big Mike, "Maybe you need another drink."

Debbie ignored the tension and turned to respond to Lucy. "I don't know him. But he's cute."

"You think? Not my type," Lucy said. "But I liked her shoes. She must get a discount."

Mike spoke up again, looking at Nancy, "You're right about one thing."

"What's that?"

"I do need another drink."

"Really?" Melanie seemed disappointed in her husband. "I thought we switched to club soda?"

Mike chided her, "When you say 'we,' do you mean you and me, you and everyone else, or just you and the pope?"

"I meant you, ya jackass."

Mike kept his tone serious. "Let me ask you this: Do you want to go home yet?"

Mike's question could be heard by the whole table and was met with silence. Music thumped from the jukebox. The game flashed on the TV screens. A murmur of conversation was heard from other parts of the Saloon. But the group suddenly remembered why they were there, and without speaking the fact aloud, no one wanted to go home.

Nancy got the group back into talking, "I figured it out."

"Thank God. What did you figure out?" asked Debbie.

Nancy explained, sort of: "Why they came in late but left early."

Lucy asked, "Who?"

"The shoe girl and the muscle man," answered Nancy.

Melanie asked, "Okay, so why did they come in late and leave early?"

"Movie date. First the movie, then the after-movie drink. The digestif, if you will."

There was a collective 'ahh' from Melanie, Debbie and Frank, who added, "Makes sense."

But Lucy asked, "Dee-jest-eef? Is that a foreign

movie?"

Nancy hoped Lucy was kidding, but Frank knew better. He said to his wife, "Stop trying to make sense, you'll hurt somebody."

To help avoid any bickering, Melanie jumped in to ask the group, "What's playing at the movie theater?"

"Movies," answered Mike.

Melanie hung her head at Mike, "You sure you don't want to go play pool?"

Frank added, "Or play in traffic."

Mike retorted, "Traffic? In Babel. That couldn't get a guy killed."

Mike's unfortunate comment hung in mid-air like a hammer above the table.

When Melanie spoke up, saying, "Right. It is time for another drink," it was like the hammer slammed on to the table. The seven others all spoke up with their agreement and, as if summoned by the imagined call to order, Dennis and Chuck emerged from the back room.

Dennis announced, "Chuck's buying. Well, for me anyway. Don't want to say I kicked his ass…"

"No, you don't. I scratched on the eight ball. That's no ass kicking."

Dennis retorted, "A W's still a W."

Beth chimed in, "And an A is always an A."

Dennis looked hurt, "What's that mean?"

"It means you've been gone long enough." Beth winked at her husband. "Go tell the waitress we need another round."

But like magic, Marilu was suddenly at the table, saying, "Sounds like y'all want another round. Pitcher of beer? Carafe of white? What about you, Mr. Cosmo? Care for another yet?"

Mike knew she was being playful, so he didn't mind. He really wanted to respond that he hadn't had a first 'yet' yet, but he didn't think she'd understand that he was being playful, too. "As a matter of fact, I'd love one. Just like the first two, but this time, I'd like it in a rocks glass."

Lucy nudged Nancy, "You ever wonder why it's called a rocks glass?"

Marilu heard her and said, "That's so funny. Someone else was asking the same thing earlier. I better find out the answer. Might come in handy." Marilu headed back to the bar.

Nancy looked after her. "Might."

"Or might not," added Debbie, in her own playful tone. "It does sounds like something one ought to know."

"Ought," said Nancy.

"Or ought not," echoed Debbie.

Mike smiled at the game. "You mean naught. I think."

Debbie returned his smile, "I think not."

It wasn't long before Marilu was back with the drinks, delivering the carafe of wine to Nancy at one head of the table and the pitcher of beer to Frank now at the other head, where he was flanked by Dennis and Chuck who sat alongside each of their wives. Marilu made a special trip again just to deliver a Cosmopolitan on the rocks to Mike.

Over the next thirty minutes, the group enjoyed their drinks and peppered the small talk with fewer acerbic comments. The cumulative effect of the alcohol was definitely mellowing them out. Anecdotes and memories began to be shared – some featuring Paul and Jenny, some not. But now, if anyone needed to mention Paul, it was done without hesitation.

Despite the late hour, none of the group was interested in going home. That act of ending the day bore a sense of completion they weren't ready for. If conversation would begin to peter out, one of them would heroically chime in with some new observation or memory or opinion, just to keep the night "alive."

Around 11:45, they all noticed yet another couple entering the Saloon. It was a well-dressed man and woman in their early forties, but the shoulder shrugs, puckered lower lips and slight head shakes among the group indicated that no one seemed to know who the couple was.

"It's nearly midnight. Who goes out at midnight?" whined Lucy.

As the woman took to her bar stool, she leaned up on the bar and kissed the bartender. Chuck and Dennis zoomed in on the woman's tight skirt as she posed for a moment on her bar stool, smoothing the skirt with her hand.

Frank noted, "Well it sure looks like the bartender knows them."

Dennis joked, "Maybe that's why it's called Tongues. Come in at midnight and get a free tongue kiss."

"It's not midnight yet," said Beth. "This day ain't over."

Barbara, who had been mostly quiet throughout the night, leaned forward and commented, "People sure slip in and out of this place all night long."

"Who does?" asked Chuck.

Big Mike answered him, "Slippery people, that's who."

"People like us?" asked Debbie.

"No slippery-er," smiled Beth.

"Seriously," whined Lucy again, "Who comes out this late?"

Frank spoke down the length of the table to his wife. "Movie date. Late show."

Chuck said, half-jokingly, "No way. They're married."

Melanie took offense, "What! Married people can't go on movie dates?"

"Married people don't go to the movies then out for a drink," Mike said matter-of-factly. "After the movie, they go home and ignore each other."

Debbie observed, "They're not married. If they were married, they wouldn't be sitting so close."

Barbara agreed, "If they were married, she wouldn't be climbing into his lap like that."

Chuck countered his wife, "They must be married,

otherwise he'd be slipping her a dollar bill about now."

It was Dennis' time to weigh in. "What she's doing on that stool… if they were married, she'd be expecting to get a new washer and dryer." That comment earned him a kick under the table from Beth.

Lucy slapped the table. "Really. Who goes out at midnight?"

Ignoring her, Frank spoke up, wanting to keep up with the jokes. "If they were married, they would still be outside with her telling him where to park."

Each joke was receiving requisite smiles, but no big laughs, until Nancy spoke up, "Okay, so they're not married. To each other."

Over everyone's laughter, Chuck clapped his hands. "Now we're talking."

"Are we? Who's talking to you?" Barbara's comment to her husband wiped the smile, and the leer, right off his face, much to the amusement of Dennis.

"How y'all doing? Can I get anyone anything?" Marilu was back at the table, her timing once again uncanny.

Melanie asked politely, "Do you serve coffee?"

"We sure do," Marilu said with a wink and a smile. "In fact, I always put on a pot at midnight. We like to take good care of our customers. We want y'all to come back safe and sound."

Under his breath, Mike muttered, "I guess no one's dying to come here."

Debbie looked at him somberly, "It's how we got here."

Lucy blurted out, to Marilu, "The couple at the bar. Doesn't look like they're having coffee."

Marilu turned to see what was going on behind her. "Oh, the Reilly's? Nah, they're great. We know them."

Mike looked up at Marilu. "I see that Mr. Reilly is enjoying himself a martini. Big run on martini glasses tonight?"

Marilu gave him a little wave. "You're right. That's

funny. We like never use those glasses."

Melanie put a mock consoling hand on her husband's shoulder. "But Mike, he's drinking a martini. You're just drinking Cosmos."

Mike defended himself, "Same difference."

"Happy you think so." Surprisingly, Melanie picked up Mike's hand and kissed it.

Beth whispered to Dennis, "I hate that expression."

"What expression?"

Marilu started to take the group's orders for coffee. Mike ordered tea.

Beth ordered a coffee then turned again to Dennis. "Same difference. Drives me nuts."

"Why?"

"I don't know. It doesn't sound proper. Like 'six of one, half a dozen of another.' Just drives me nuts."

"Doesn't bother me," said Dennis, adding, just to annoy his wife, "To me, it don't make no never mind."

"You know you're insufferable."

"Yep." Waving to Marilu, Dennis said, "No coffee for me. I'd like another beer. If they're not ordering a pitcher, I'll just take a bottle."

Beth was still annoyed, "Really?"

Dennis shrugged, "I'm not driving."

"Or anything else."

Dennis shrugged again, "Okay. Whatever that means."

Marilu left the group with an order for seven coffees – all decaf – one tea (if she could find a teabag, "No promises.") and two bottles of beer, for Dennis and Chuck.

"So, what do you think we can expect for a cuppa Joe in this place?" Debbie asked her friends.

Frank admitted, "I'd have very low expectations."

Lucy sniped, "You would."

Nancy countered, "Actually, I'm thinking it will be great. You got to figure that the Saloon gets a decent-sized trucker crowd. They need a good java."

"Like the guy at the bar. In the camouflage hat." Frank turned on the sarcasm. "He looks like a regular gourmet coffee connoisseur."

Nancy said, "Well, I don't think he's ordering decaf."

"I bet he's ordering a Harvey Wallbanger," guessed Lucy.

Melanie guessed, "Or a Rusty Nail."

"Definitely not a Grasshopper or a Pink Lady," joked Debbie.

Frank weighed in, "Maybe a Sidecar or a Rob Roy."

Barbara admitted, "I've never had any of those drinks. I can't imagine what's in them."

"You know, one time when we all go out," suggested Beth, "we should all order different drinks with funny names and do a taste test."

Lucy made a face to convey her disgust at the idea, "Oh I'm sure we'd all throw up."

Mike turned to Beth and laughed, "When we all go out? When was the last time all of us went out?"

Not to be dismissed, Beth corrected him, "Not the last time, the next time."

Mike guffawed. "Next time? I'll be dead by then."

Beth really wanted to give it to him, "Then maybe that's the reason we'll all get together."

Mike lowered his voice, "If you do, don't come here."

"Cosmo that bad?" chided Debbie.

Nancy asked, "Don't like the jukebox?"

Melanie elbowed her husband, "Scared of the waitress?" That got a laugh from all. Save Mike, who waited a beat.

"No. This was Paul's place."

That brought the heavy silence back down upon the table.

Mike felt badly; he didn't mean to be morose, he was being honest and respectful of Paul. To break the icy mood he just created, Mike opened up, "When I die, you should all go to the movies."

The group all thought about this comment and then their own last wishes as Marilu returned and set down seven cups of coffee. "Still checking for a tea bag," she said to Mike. "I'll be back with the beers."

Melanie tried to gauge her husband Mike's seriousness about going to the movies as a memorial. "Do you really expect us to sit in the dark and think about you?"

His only response was an arched eyebrow.

Debbie leaned forward. "It would have to be a comedy. A bad one."

Frank jumped in from the end of the table. "No, it would be a disaster movie."

"How about a horror movie?" Everyone laughed, surprised that the comment came from Melanie.

Mike looked at her, "Really? Living with me is such a horror?"

She smiled, "You'd be dead. Living *without* you would be a horror." Looking up at the ceiling, as if pondering the concept, Melanie added, "Maybe. Maybe not."

Feigning disappointment in his wife, Mike turned to his right and asked Beth. "What do you think it should be?"

She looked away, laughing. "I don't know. Have they made any gay westerns?"

Everyone burst out laughing, even Mike.

During the outburst, Debbie noticed one of the other patrons – the young white man who had been sitting with the three older black women – dash by the table and duck into the men's room. She thought his movement looked highly suspicious and commented, "That was weird."

Frank noticed him too, but brushed it off, "Hey, when you gotta go, you gotta go."

Debbie said, "He looked like he wanted to skip town."

Barbara spoke up, "I think I know why."

"Why's that?" asked Chuck.

"I think his friends are a little inebriated."

The group cautiously turned to watch the three women from the supermarket cautiously stand up at their table and begin a slow and unsteady stroll towards the front door. The women looked sheepish and embarrassed, and one looked especially drunk. They muttered a few 'good nights' as they walked out. Nancy offered a friendly, "Good night, ladies. Home safe now."

Frank uttered, "Good night, Irene."

"Which one's Irene?" asked Chuck.

Frank looked at him, incredulously. To tweak him, Frank said, matter-of-factly, "The tall one."

Marilu returned with two bottles of beer, but before she set them down in front of Dennis and Chuck, she asked, in a very friendly way, "You aren't driving tonight, gentlemen. Are you?"

Beth piped up, a tad defensively to Dennis' ear, "Don't you worry, we'll take good care of them." Then she added quietly, for Barbara's benefit, "They're lucky if we let them get in the car."

Dennis chimed in, "I hope those ladies who just left weren't driving. They looked over-served."

"Nah, they'll be fine. Before he left, their boss called for a cab."

Frank told Marilu, "He didn't leave."

She was surprised, "He didn't?"

"Nope. He's in the men's room," Debbie noted. "We think he's hiding."

It was Chuck who said, "No, he's not. He's playing darts."

Marilu turned from the table to investigate. She was gone only a few minutes, but when she emerged from the back room, Frank thought she looked annoyed. As she passed by, she said to no one in particular, "Still thirsty, and still fresh."

The group watched her head back to the bar, but halfway there, she stopped and spun around.

Startled, Debbie uttered, "Hunh."

Marilu marched back to the table and spoke very politely to Big Mike. "I am so sorry, but we simply could not find a single tea bag. Would you care for a decaf?"

"That's okay," Mike responded. "Thanks for looking. I will take a Coke though."

Again, Melanie challenged her husband, "Really? You want the caffeine."

"Oh, I need it."

"One Coca-Cola coming up," chirped Marilu.

After she left, Melanie teased Big Mike. "From fruity drinks to soda pop, they got you covered here at the Saloon."

The front door suddenly opened, and the group was surprised to see a police officer enter, take a quick look around, then casually take a seat at the bar. The bartender immediately greeted him with a friendly handshake and jovial utterances.

"What's with the cop?" asked Chuck.

"That's a highway patrolman," noted Frank.

Debbie suggested, "Looks like a regular."

Mike said, "Well, I hope he's not interested in a Cosmo. He's going to be disappointed."

That cracked up the group again, and their laughter drew the attention of the policeman. He gave them a general nod of the head. In response, all the women, and Frank, toasted him with their cups of coffee and broad smiles.

Dennis muttered, "Good thing I'm not driving."

"Good thing," muttered Beth in response, "since we're still indoors."

Marilu came by with Mike's Coke, but then delivered a large glass of ice water to the back room. She reappeared very quickly.

"Marilu?" Frank called her over to the table. "It's time we settled up. Do you mind bringing us the check?"

"Sure thing. I'll be just a minute."

Since they were all looking at him, Frank decided to address the group. "Friends, I think it's time we call it a day."

Chuck clapped his hands. "Show's over. Nothing left to see."

"It has been a long day," Barbara said.

Nancy moaned, "God I feel like the funeral was… days ago."

But Debbie said, "It feels like an hour ago to me."

Mike stared at her, "I don't think I ever left it."

Melanie put out her hand as if to stop the direction of the conversation. "Look. We're all going to wake up tomorrow. The sun will be shining. We'll get out of bed, and we'll go about our day."

Lucy blurted out, "It's supposed to rain tomorrow."

"If we do anything tomorrow, we should do something for Jenny." It was Beth, once again keeping the group grounded.

Frank said, "I'm sure the sun won't be shining for her tomorrow."

"She buried her sunshine today." Debbie couldn't shake her sorrow.

But Lucy blurted out again, "It's supposed to rain tomorrow."

"Okay, we get it," snapped Frank from across the table.

Mike said, matter-of-factly, "You don't need a weather man to know which way the wind blows."

"Thanks Bob," said Melanie, her voice betraying disappointment that Mike couldn't let pass any opportunity to be witty.

Marilu returned with the check. "Thank you everyone. That last round, the one before the coffees, that one was on Tongue. He said 'thanks for stopping in.' Who wants the damage?"

"That was very nice of him." Debbie spoke with authority. "Frank, you take the check and divvy it up. You're our math man."

"I'm a science teacher," Frank complained. "Let Dennis do it, he's the accountant."

Beth quipped, "I don't think Mr. CPA can count his

toes about now."

"I resent that. I think." Dennis was aware that his tongue was a little thick.

"Give it here. I'll work it out." The check was passed over to Nancy who got to work calculating a generous tip and then dividing the total among the five couples.

Very quietly, without being overt or obvious, Frank and Lucy, Debbie, Melanie, Beth, and Barbara, each looked around the Saloon. They each thought of Paul. And Jenny. Some pictured them in the Saloon from memory, some through their imagination.

Only Frank noticed the young Suprette manager sneak out of the back room and quietly exit the Saloon.

Dennis stared at the remaining mouthful of beer in his glass, wondering if he was in trouble with his wife.

Chuck stared at Marilu's ass as she leaned on the bar talking with Tongue.

Mike closed his eyes and said a prayer. The song on the jukebox sang about 'home,' and Mike wanted to be there.

Nancy announced, "Our number's up. We're good to go."

Tongue's Tale 8

I'll tell you how I lost my tongue. Being a good neighbor, that's how. I used to live next to Millie Murchinson. And her cat. A big fat orange cat named Sunshine. I mean this cat was huge. Anyway, one summer afternoon I hear Millie calling for me from her backyard. She sounded upset, so I go running out back. It's hot as Hades and I was wearing just shorts and sandals. No shirt. I'm dripping with sweat because my air conditioner was on the fritz. "Millie, Millie, what's the matter?" I ask her. "Oh, it's Sunshine," she says. "He's got himself stuck up in the tree." I look up and lo and behold, there's fatso perched in this tree like the Cheshire Cat, only this one ain't smiling. "Do you mind climbing up to rescue Sunshine?" she says. I tell her I can't climb no tree. But of course, she has a ladder for me to use. Anyway, up I go, and of course, I have to go to the very top rung. I can barely reach Sunshine, so I make one valiant effort. I throw my arm up and as soon as I feel fur, I snatch it. Well, this doesn't make Sunshine too happy. As I'm pulling the cat down to safety, it comes down with all its claws out, flailing like a drowning man. I got cut up pretty good, all across my chest and back. Damn cat then jumps off of me, lands safely and then waddles off as if nothing happened. And what happens to me? Damn ladder slips, I fall to the ground, landing on a damn garden hoe that Millie had been swinging to coax the cat down. That hoe cut off the tip of my tongue. But I've got no complaints. Could have been my nose. Then where would I be?

BURNING DOWN THE HOUSE
(10:00 PM)

One drink in and I'm already itching to write. Maybe it's nostalgia. Maybe it's knowing what's going to happen. I think a lot about fate, but I don't put much weight in it. A man's got to control his own destiny. But sometimes I think fate put this pencil in my hand.

This pencil. I like writing that out, with this pencil. Strange. To be a thing. A simple inanimate object. But to move and function too. Of course, it can't do anything without my hand.

It's an instrument. And that's what I feel like. Even tonight. I'm this inanimate object, just an instrument. But I wonder whose hand I'm in. I need control.

I just ordered another and the bartender didn't bother me with the usual bullshit questions about where I'm from and what's with the notebook. Smart guy. I wonder how long he's been here. Wasn't here 20 years ago, that's for sure. I wonder if any of these folk were here back then and stuck around anyway. Happens sometimes that little towns like this clear out when something happens.

Would really like to know, but it's not the kind of thing I could ask, is it? If the town did change, then maybe that's why it happened. The first time. Here. A town called Babel. So I'd never forget. That would be fate.

And I was the instrument.
Still am. Still. Am.

❀

Waitress just asked if I wanted to order something from the kitchen. She's cute. Quite a body. Nice smile. Seems real nice. But I've been all across the country and you meet so many cute waitresses who all seem nice. They're all the same. Would be a helluva better world if everyone could be that nice and be for real.

❀

Empty bar in an empty town. Four guys in the back, probably playing pool. Couple on a date staring more at the game than at each other. They should be nervous. If I catch musclehead look at me again with his condescending I Am The Man, I'm going to go over there and smack his girlfriend and then just be done with this place.
Yeah. That's control.
Sometimes this pencil saves lives.

❀

Next round, I'm going to drink real slow. Like this is the longest night of my life. Longest = last. Lastest. Last-test. Latest. The late great.
Greatest.

❀

Strange group sitting at a long table. Don't fit the place. Don't fit with each other. A bunch of couples. Some of the husbands or boyfriends are the ones playing pool. Except for the one guy who was sitting at the bar. They got him to go play in the back. That's why I'm all alone here. Better for me.
They'll say fate brought them together. But what fate

brought them here to this place on this night? It's the Saturday night of Labor Day weekend. Fate did not send them away for vacation. And now only I know what fate awaits them. Only I know.

Who knows what fate awaits me? Did it change since the first time I was here? Did I control it? Did I change it? Am I an instrument of change? Or just control.

This is a good drink. I feel very clear-headed tonight. I made the right decision, coming back here to end this. I'm completing a circle, in both time and space. Twenty years of one long circle. Wish I could see it on a map. Mark all the places I've stayed, all the places I've changed, then all the places I moved on to. But that would be stupid, because if anyone found that kind of map, I'd be caught. And I've never been caught because I have been smart. Smarter. I understand it.

Even when it's not on a road, cars always crash at the intersections of people's lives.

I love to sip my drink so slow. I imagine it's the last drink of water on earth and I'll never sip anything again. I'm afraid of the thirst that will kill me. A desert planet. All alone. The last man on earth, dying of thirst. No one there to give me a drink. To save me. I must drink slowly, make it last. I close my eyes and feel the liquid race right into my veins, shooting throughout my body. My blood turning bright red. My cells springing to life. My brain exploding with understanding.

I opened my eyes and saw the waitress staring at me. She seemed concerned. I guess I might have scared her, sitting here with my eyes closed, sipping my whiskey like a beggar. I smiled back at her to say I was okay, but she didn't notice. She went over to take care of the three black women sitting with a white guy. They're in their forties, he's not even 30. That I can't figure. Some perverse fate has brought them here.

I sit. I think. I sip. I think. I sit and watch. I watch and remember. I sip some more. I write. I am. I am right. I sip and I am sure.

Even though it's not crowded, these fated ones are spread out. Won't be easy like I imagined. Let me re-imagine it again. One more round. Round. Around. All around me. All a round. Me. How many rounds?

I usually like to watch the action behind the bar, but this place is dull. I don't think this bartender knows how to do more than fill a pitcher of beer. But he keeps his distance.

Those black women keep playing crap on the jukebox I don't want to hear. I've got music in my head that I need to hear.

Bartender looks like he's making his first cocktail. Might never have held a shaker before. I think he's just a kid. But he's older than the waitress. They've got something going. I can tell. I know so much about people.

Guy just came back from playing pool. Looks embarrassed. Sloppy. Hope he's not driving far. Keep him off the road. That's right, pay your tab and hit the road. Wake up tomorrow with a hangover, hear the news, and throw up all the guilt of the world.

The more I sit here, the more I boil. The volcano no one suspects. But more of them leave. Fleeing to safety without even knowing it. F A T E. Goodbye people.

❀

Gentleman. Gentle man. Calling for a taxi to safely drive his lady friends home. Gentleman my ass. Responsibility for one's actions defines Character. This kid's a punk.

Those women are all drunk. The scrawny one is a mess. Disgrace. Not the way to act in public. I wonder what white boy said to that good looking one. She looked pretty nasty about him getting so close. I wouldn't mind getting that close. But not to a nasty one like that. No woman is worth a damn thing in the world. Leave me in peace.

❀

So much for my final solitude. Rich couple shows up and starts dry humping at the bar. Animals. Where is the control? Man needs to control his urges. Women are sin. S I N F U L

I see the word w-i-c-k-e-d in the ice cubes in my glass. But when I drink it I only taste w-h-i-s-k-e-y.

One more glass of wickedness barkeep please. The night is getting late.

❀

I'm just sitting here scribbling in my book, minding my own business. Now there's a cop at the bar. He's everybody's friend. Too bad. Everybody is somebody's friend, and everybody still dies. If you're here for me, you're too late. I am already gone.

The dogs in heat have left leaving their stench of sex and money. God damn. I want to hunt them down. Animals.

You can get drunk just looking at those women leave the bar. Good riddance to yesterday's trash.

You must be worthy of Fate for Fate to pick you.

20 years ago, he was worthy. I picked him just like how Fate picked me. He chose that gas station. I chose that gas station. That was our Fate. I was worthy then and I am worthy now. Tonight. Full circle.

Sometimes I believe he is still waiting for me. IN THE NIGHT. I am not afraid. I carry Judgment with me. It sings quietly to me from below this bar stool where I sit, getting ready. When Judgment speaks tonight, its voice will be loud. VOICE OF THUNDER.

Cop's gone. There goes the misbegotten hero. IF ONLY HE KNEW. That's what he'll tell them. And he'll still be saying it when he retires. Mumbling to himself about the FATE he was dealt. (The only FATE he was worthy of.)

Cop should go after the white boy stud who snuck out like a dog with his tail between his legs. Arrest him for something he was thinking of. Don't mind the police. Mind the police. Mind Police.

Last call says the bartender. Not for me. FOR YOU ALL.

WAIT.

The voice called to me and I waited. I stilled my hand, like Abraham over Isaac. Alas I succumb to that voice. My hand was already on the metal when I heard her. Destruction sits at my feet quiet again like a loyal dog. Because of HER VOICE.

It was the jukebox that stopped me. That sweet voice that I never thought I'd hear again found me. If you ripped me open and paged through everything in my heart it would have taken a lifetime to find those words again. HER VOICE sang them again tonight. And I cannot KILL. Not here, not now.

I am not upset. But how did this happen?

I know now: that waitress played one last song. I heard her tell the bartender that it was her mother's favorite. I won't tell her it's mine. I'll ask her her name and write it down it my book once I'm outside in my truck with my gun lying cold in the seat next to me.

Strangers brush shoulders and never see how the other person's next step may take a different path because of that one moment shared unknowingly.

That girl has spared this town a dozen more deaths, and me, the fate of this night.

Tongue's Tale 9

If anyone ever dares you to chew broken glass, don't.

THIS MUST BE THE PLACE (1:30 AM)

Tongue turned off the orangey red neon sign that burnished the word SALOON on the roof of the two-story building and locked the front door. He ambled back behind the bar and poured a glass of amaretto over ice for Marilu and shot a fresh spray of tonic into the pint glass he had sipped on throughout the night. He turned off the two televisions and slid under the counter leaf and plopped down on a bar stool.

Marilu finished wiping down the tables, turned off the overhead lights and slid onto a bar stool next to Tongue. They sat facing each other, their knees interlocked but not touching. Marilu raised her glass, "Thanks, baby."

"Some night." Tongue clinked her glass with his.

"You're telling me."

"Full moon?"

"I don't think so."

"Holiday weekend?" Tongue smirked, "Not that Labor Day is really that interesting."

"Maybe. It was just one strange Saturday night. The old stand-bys. A couple of newbies. That table of 10."

Tongue laughed. "Some wild cards to boot."

"You're telling me."

"Yeah, I am." Tongue winked at her.

They sipped their drinks looking at each other like it was a staring contest.

"How'd we do?" asked Marilu.

"Pretty good. Tips were up. Think it's the logo shirt I

make you wear?" Tongue was proud of his branding brainstorm, with its Rolling Stones-like tongue logo. But he was only kidding. For one thing, the logo wasn't very visible on the t-shirt, because the shirt was too big on Marilu's petite frame.

Marilu teased back. "I'm sure it's how you make me wear it. Tight and tied like I'm some..."

"Don't even say it. You know I'm not like that. I'm a prude through and through."

"Oh yeah? How'd you lose the tip of your tongue?"

"Devilish girl tonight, aincha?" Tongue pushed her knee.

Marilu smiled. "So, *my* tips were good?"

"Yep. The big group was generous."

"I'm not surprised. Mr. Francis was my science teacher and Mrs. Black taught English. I had her a couple of times. She was my favorite. All-time favorite. She is wicked funny."

Tongue sipped his tonic. "I kept looking over there, trying to figure out who belonged to who. They kept changing seats."

"I'm pretty sure I figured it out. You just had to watch how they bickered with each other, usually in a funny way. The ones who were meanest to each other were the married ones."

"Hunh. You think we'll get like that."

Marilu looked at Tongue and said sincerely, "Only if that's your idea of a proposal."

Tongue actually blushed. After another sip, he decided to change the subject. "So, what did you learn tonight?"

"I learned that our boy Carl is serious with his shoe store girlfriend. I learned that Jim Helper – who's a pig, but who's surprised? – is going to have a rough day at work tomorrow, or whenever."

"Why's that?"

"Well, he's the one who kept buying those women drinks and I'm sure that they'll be hurting in the morning.

They're either calling in sick or will be pissed off at him all day. It'll be fun to stop by the supermarket and see if he's working a cash register."

Tongue put his glass down on the bar. "So, what's the deal with my buddy Carl?"

"Mr. Fever looks like he's got a crush, and I think it's mutual. They look kind of sweet for each other, as they say."

"How so?"

"When I called him Mr. Fever like you told me to, she lit up. I think she liked the idea of him having a secret nickname."

"Yeah, all chicks dig that stuff," Tongue said with a big smile.

"Oh, I'm sure you're right, Mr. Thomas T. Thomas."

Tongue put his index finger to his lips, kissed it, then tapped it on the tip of Marilu's nose.

She asked him, "So what did you learn tonight?"

"I'm excited to say I learned how to make a Cosmopolitan. Not sure if I'll ever need to make one again. Do you like them?"

"They're okay. The guy drinking them, he was funny. I want to say queer, but not in that way. An odd duck."

"As opposed to an even duck?"

"No, as opposed to an even Steven."

"I see." Tongue laughed as he thought to himself, 'I better look that one up. Might come in handy next time I meet a Steven.'

Marilu slapped his knee. "Hey, what was with the trucker at the end of the bar? Creepy or what?"

"Yeah, I gave him some thought. Definitely never saw him before. Didn't seem like he was from around here, but at the same time he seemed very comfortable. Did you see him scribbling in his little notebook?"

"Was that what he was doing?"

"Yeah, but I have no idea what he was writing down. Pretty intense guy. I made a point of not offering him too many refills. He must have sat there four hours, nursing four whiskeys. And you know what?"

"What?"

"Never went to the bathroom." Tongue gave her an exaggerated look of shock.

"No way."

"Well, I didn't see him go."

Marilu laughed, "Do you think he was wearing one of those trucker's friends?"

"God, I hope not."

"Wait a minute. He did go. Just as the big table was heading out, he ducked into the men's room carrying his duffel bag. *What was with the bag?* Why didn't he leave it in his car or truck or whatever?"

"Must have been valuable."

"A duffel?" Marilu was incredulous.

"I mean whatever was inside. Like a gold bar."

"Gold bar. You think?" Now she was just sarcastic.

"Well, the way he carried it, it was heavy."

"And a little long. Like a telescope."

"That's it!" Tongue poked her knee. "He was a trucker astronomer. And he was writing down everyone's signs."

"That would make him an astrologer not an astronomer."

"That too."

Marilu smiled at Tongue and took a mouthful of amaretto. "What else did you learn?"

"The Reillys spent a month in Europe, don't ask where. I'm sure it was everywhere."

"I'd like to go to Europe someday."

Tongue sat up tall on his bar stool. "Well, play your cards right young lady and maybe one day your dream will come true."

"Not on tips from high school teachers," groaned Marilu.

"You mean, like 'Study hard and stay in school.'"

Marilu ignored the joke. "Did you see that kid Colin Hunter? He's going off to graduate school."

"Good for him. Kid deserves every break he can get. It's one thing to grow up without a dad, but to know your father was gunned down while your mother's pregnant with you. Wasn't even a robbery. Just a thrill kill. That's what the police said. That's tough."

Marilu sipped her drink. "Tougher for his mother, don't you think? I'll never understand why she stayed around."

"Home. It's all about home."

"What do you mean?" asked Marilu.

"It's where people want to be." Tongue reached over and put his hand on Marilu's knee. "Gasoline Peggy and her husband picked Babel to be the home for their new family. For their future. For the rest of their lives. She never left because this was where their home was going to be. She stayed because she stayed true to their decision." He leaned back again. "I'm sure it was hard to do, and that's why it's the greatest example of love I've ever heard of."

Marilu looked at Tongue, seeing yet another deeper side to him. She thought, 'I do like this man.' She finished her drink and slid off the bar stool to stand between Tongue's knees. She put her arms up around his neck. "Can I show you another example?" Not waiting for a reply, she leaned up and kissed him, her open mouth sharing the sweet almond taste of her drink.

After a few moments, their faces parted, and they looked longingly into each other's eyes.

Finally, Marilu spoke up. "So. Learn anything else tonight, Mr. Tongue?"

"Yeah, I snuck it onto the jukebox when I came in today. 'Meant To Be' by Mary Fahl. I love it too, you know."

She started to sing it to Tongue in a whispery voice:

"Life is hard
Sometimes it leaves you scarred
Too many lonely hours in the night
When all your faith is gone
If you can just hold on
You may get one more chance to make it right."

Tongue whispered in response, "That's not the part that caught my attention. I think it ends something like: *I still believe in love and there must be a God above because he brought me you."*

He leaned forward and kissed Marilu. When he pulled away, he admitted, "It's a pretty song, but I didn't take you as a sucker for such a simple melody."

"Oh, don't be so naïve," Marilu said. "The melody is catchy and all, but it's the lyrics. It's always about the lyrics. It's always about what people say to each other. You just have to listen."

Tongue's Tale 10

The love of my life caught me in a lie once. It was an embarrassing, pitiful lie. I can't even repeat it. Well, the tip of my tongue just fell off. Out of shame.

KEVIN JOHN WINDORF

Born and raised in New York City, Kevin John Windorf attended New York University and Fordham College, where he studied creative writing, poetry, and film production. While pursuing a career in communications, he has written extensively in a wide range of creative formats including screenplays, short fiction, and poetry.

In 2013, his short story "Call from The Cabin" was featured on NPR's "All Things Considered" as a program favorite from its Three Minute Fiction contest #10.

Samples of Kevin's work can be found at
www.kevinwindorf.com.

www.ingramcontent.com/pod-product-compliance
Lightning Source LLC
Chambersburg PA
CBHW051251170626
46809CB00004B/1595